MW01688152

BISHOP'S GAMBIT

Samara Knight

AURION PRESS

ISBN: 978-1-7382539-8-2 (Ebook)
ISBN: 978-1-7382539-7-5 (Paperback)

First edition November 2024

For those who began as adversaries
and grew into lovers

Dear Amy
Thank you so much

AUTHOR'S NOTE

Bishop's Gambit is a romantic reimagining of an espionage graphic novel series first published in 2010. Originally set in the year 2026, today's world has diverged from the novel's vision. In response, I've taken the challenge to 'rewrite the future' and retell the story of Helix and Bishop from a more contemporary worldview.

This book is primarily set in Hong Kong and the UK, where British spelling is used.

This book contains adult themes (18+), sexually explicit scenes, and acts of violence.

For additional information and backstory, please visit samara-knight.com or say hello @samaraknightauthor.

AGENCIES, REGIMENTS AND ALLIANCES IN 'BISHOP'S GAMBIT'

SIS (popularly known as 'MI6')
UK's Secret Intelligence Service

SVR (Sluzhba for short)
Neo-Soviet Foreign Intelligence Service

Guoanbu
China's State Security Ministry, responsible for domestic, international, and counter-intelligence

BND
Germany's Federal Intelligence Service

SRR (Special Reconnaissance Regiment)
British Army unit specialising in covert surveillance and reconnaissance missions

Red Pact (红公约 / красный пакт)
An alliance between the Union of Neo-Soviet Republics (UNSR) and the People's Republic of China, formed as a formidable counterweight to the Allies in 2030

Spying is like a game of chess: Sometimes you have to withdraw, sometimes you have to sacrifice one of your pieces to win—preferably a knight rather than a king or queen.

John Rhys-Davies

0 / THE END

// Moscow, Union of Neo-Soviet Republics, 2036 //

The city's lights glittered against the cold night, casting long, haunting shadows across the military hospital. Hidden deep within the fifth floor, where the corridors were tight and the air was thick with antiseptic, Bishop found her sanctuary in the darkness. She crouched low in a forgotten corner, the faint hum of fluorescent lights from the hall the only sound breaking the stillness.

Her fingers worked quickly, but with the precision of a surgeon, as she prepared the ampoule—a small, glass vial containing a deadly elixir.

Tonight, everything will end.

Her thoughts lingered on those words, a promise to herself, to the mission, to the dark allure of her profession. She slipped the syringe into her coat and melted back into the darkness, her movements as smooth as silk, a ghost in the night, ready to strike.

1 / PROXY

// Burdenko Military Hospital //

In the sterile corridors of the hospital's fifth floor, each step echoed faintly in the quiet. Bishop, known only to few by her real name, moved with the grace of someone who had danced with death one too many times.

The stark white walls seemed to pulse with an eerie tranquility, a sharp contrast to the activities on the lower floors and the world outside, where Moscow was slowly awakening under the early spring drizzle.

Her augmented glasses displayed a translucent blueprint of the hospital, the crisp lines guiding her through the maze. Each corner she turned brought her closer to her target, General Zaitsev. His position was marked just a few doors ahead, and she could already feel her muscles coiling, ready for whatever might come next.

Just as she was about to cross the final stretch, a sharp pulse of crimson flared across her vision, her screen flashing with urgent text:

NEWTON TO BISHOP
ABORT OP
RETURN TO PONDS ASAP

Her brow furrowed in confusion. Why? She was seconds away from the objective. As she pondered the sudden directive, she saw him.

The mysterious man emerged from the opposite end of the corridor and casually passed her. His raven hair and white coat mirrored her disguise, but his piercing blue eyes struck her with a jolt of recognition that was both alarming and strangely compelling.

Ignoring the abort command, she quickened her pace towards the VIP room. Swiping her ID, she entered to find a luxurious room where General Zaitsev lay on a bed, an oxygen mask over his face. To her dismay, the heart monitor's screen flickered with a faint green line. Someone had gotten to her target first.

Rushing out, she replayed the brief encounter with the mysterious man just now. He stirred memories of an operative from a past mission in Cairo. Visions of a grey chamber, in a briefing with men in black uniforms, came to her mind.

She shot into the main hallway. Two staff members chatted near the elevators as she caught sight of the man again, by the emergency exit. He glanced at her, his eyes remaining just a moment too long, before he vanished through the door.

Bishop barrelled after him. The staircase loomed ahead. She caught sight of him on the next floor up, moving with extraordinary speed, his every motion assured and commanding. As she climbed, her thoughts raced back to Cairo and the grey chamber.

He had looked different then. Blond. Aloof. Pretty.

But she was certain it was him, a figure who seemed to lead her towards a future she couldn't ignore.

The stairs didn't turn out to be endless after all. After minutes of non-stop, heavy climbing, Bishop finally reached the door that led outside to the hospital's rooftop. She grabbed the handle and pulled it open, stepping into the cold, black night.

The city's vast expanse lay before her, glimmering skyscrapers and the majesty of the Kremlin. There was no time to appreciate the view. The chase was on.

Her gaze cut through the shadows, locking onto him. He had stripped away the disguise—no more white coat, no more dark wig to obscure him. The transformation was stark. Now he stood in a black tactical uniform that clung to his powerful frame, every sharp line of him honed for movement. A parachute backpack was strapped to his shoulders, the key to his escape.

Bishop watched as he climbed the ledge and readied to jump.

"Stop right there!" she commanded in Russian, her silver SIG steady in her hand, finger hovering over the trigger.

The man turned to face her. Fair hair whipped in the wind, catching in the glow of the city lights. His face was illuminated just enough to show the sharp planes of his cheekbones, the glint of something unreadable in his eyes. He didn't look surprised. He looked amused.

The air between them crackled. For a beat, neither of them moved… until he broke the stalemate.

A faint smile curled on his lips as he lifted a hand, miming the tip of an invisible hat. Then, without a word, he stepped off the ledge.

Bishop's heart pounded as she rushed to the edge, bending over to see him plummeting toward the dark streets below. The city lights cast eerie shadows, the dim streetlights barely illuminating the ground. She tapped the left frame of her glasses, switching to night vision.

Her fibre-optic screens shifted, the world around her transforming into shades of green and grey. She caught sight of the parachute as it deployed, a small circular object blooming in her vision. The man's dark figure, now clear against the night, descended into a desolate narrow alley.

The black waters of Patryarshy Ponds were perfectly still, a calm oasis tucked within the exclusive sprawl of Moscow's elite residential district.

Inside the one-bedroom flat, darkness reigned until Bishop pushed the door open. She flipped the switch, bathing the compact, modern space in warm light. It was exactly the way she liked it: minimalist and orderly. Her face was grim as she shrugged off her white overcoat, draping it over the back of a designer chair.

She moved to the kitchen with a determined stride, pouring herself a heavy splash of lemon vodka into soda water. Over her year-long deployment in the Union of Neo-Soviet Republics, she had developed a mild addiction to anything citrus. She gulped it down in one go, feeling better almost instantly.

Her fingers traced over her phone as she crossed into the living room, tapping a code and sending a signal to the flatscreen mounted on the wall. It flickered to life, revealing the sharp, no-nonsense face of her case officer.

"Bishop," Newton greeted with a clipped nod, his gaze steely behind an outdated brown suit. He looked English through and through, polished and stone-cold in his mannerisms.

Bishop's icy stare could have cut through steel. "What's going on, Newton?"

She spoke with a crisp and polished British accent that disguised her working-class background. She had grown up navigating multicultural southeast London, honing her skills and grit long before she joined the military. Her diction, perfected through years of mimicking and refining, was just one of the many tools in her arsenal as an intelligence operative.

"You will fly to London tomorrow for a new assignment briefing," the case officer replied, his tone as detached as ever.

"Hang on a minute. I was in the middle of an operation when you pulled me."

"It makes little difference now," Newton replied, shaking his head. "A proxy has completed the op."

Her jaw tightened. *A proxy.* "Why?"

"You have been reassigned."

Disbelief coloured her voice. "I was just about to finish up tonight. I didn't need you to send another agent to kill Zaitsev."

"We'll need you here tomorrow, Bishop."

"Do you think I cannot complete my own mission?" she challenged again, barely controlling her resentment.

"We simply need you back in London," he repeated.

Although she never liked him much, Bishop always tried to maintain a semblance of respect for Newton. This time, though, she felt like shoving his arrogance up his rear.

"Who was the proxy?" she demanded.

"You know that's classified information."

"I met him, Newton. I recognised him from a past mission. I'll know sooner or later, so just give me his name."

Newton's irritation finally seeped through his otherwise cold demeanour. "His codename is Helix. Chief Adamson saw fit to send him there. Satisfied?"

Bishop didn't respond. Her silence crackled with rage, and Newton's expression remained impassive, even as he added, "If there are no other questions, I suggest you start clearing the safehouse. Your flight leaves in six hours. Newton out."

The screen went black, leaving Bishop staring into the dim reflection of her own stormy expression. All her year-long work in Moscow had just gone out the window. She wasn't one to blame others easily, but this time, she wasn't about to let it slide.

// Vauxhall Cross //

Spring had finally arrived in southeast England, bringing mild and acceptable weather. But Bishop felt no excitement to be back in the capital.

Parking her nondescript grey car in the basement of SIS headquarters, she headed straight for the lift. She swiped her ID and rested her palm on the scanner, instantly receiving a green flash of approval.

The transparent lift doors opened and she stepped in, calling for Floor 4. The voice of the robotic operator greeted her from the speaker.

`Welcome back, Agent Bishop. The Chief awaits you in her office.`

"Thank you," she replied automatically.

In her wood-panelled office, Leonor Adamson, who looked more like a notable politician than the Chief of Special Operations Division, clasped her hands together on the table.

The room was adorned with dark mahogany furniture, a gleaming glass desk and tasteful artwork. The woman herself exuded sophisticated elegance, with her classic Chanel suit, short coiffed brown hair and matching pearl accessories.

"In the months leading up to the presidential election in China, the situation in Hong Kong has grown increasingly perilous," she began. "We've lost four of our agents, and a British family was caught in the crossfire. The timing isn't a coincidence."

Adamson retrieved three electronic folders from her drawer, placing them gently on the glass table. "The analysts have concluded that Neo-Soviet operatives are behind these incidents. Here is a list of Sluzhba agents in Hong Kong, working under an intelligence official named Kuznetsov."

She continued: "Your mission is twofold: neutralise the threat posed by these Soviet agents, and assist the Hong Kong station chief in uncovering the details behind the murders. You are authorised to use force when necessary."

The lines on her face etched with the weight of experience and the pressures of her role. "Any questions, Helix?" she inquired.

Helix, who had been quietly sitting across from Adamson, reached for the e-folders. His shoulder-length hair fell slightly over his brow, adding an air of dishevelled charm to his otherwise pristine appearance. His frame, visible beneath the tan suit, spoke volumes of his special forces background.

"What were our agents working on before their deaths?" he asked with a voice dark yet enchanting, traces of his German origins sometimes seeping through his otherwise flawless Americanised accent.

"Election monitoring," Adamson replied. "The Hong Kong station chief will fill you in."

The intercom crackled to life, breaking the silence.

`Madam. Agent Bishop is here.`

"Oh, yes. Send her in," Adamson said, turning to Helix, who was readying to leave. "You're not leaving already, are you?"

Helix's lips curved into something between a smirk and a secret. He rose smoothly, buttoning his jacket with unhurried ease. "I'll leave you to brief Bishop personally." He held Adamson's firm handshake for a beat before letting go. "Till next time, Madam."

As he moved toward the door, it slid open to reveal Bishop. She looked striking in her fitted striped suit, though a few strands of hair had escaped her ponytail. At her average height, she seemed petite compared to his towering frame, though her heels added a couple of inches. He noted her seemingly harmless femininity, a sharp contrast to the lethal operative she truly was, with a string of confirmed kills under her belt.

For a moment, they simply stared.

Bishop hadn't expected to see him again so soon. From up close, she couldn't help but notice the subtle charm he exuded—magnetic, even. His presence was disarming, with an effortless confidence that irritated as much as it unsettled her.

She had managed to put the previous night's events behind her during the early flight, but now, the grudge began to resurface. He, however, pretended not to notice her irritation, stepping slightly aside.

"Ladies first."

She narrowed her eyes and swept past him without a word. The door slid shut behind her as she faced Adamson, who smiled gently.

"Nice to see you again, Bishop," the Chief greeted, her voice warm, as though greeting an old friend.

"The pleasure's all mine, Madam," Bishop replied, taking a seat. Despite the pleasantries, the air felt charged, as if something important lingered on the edge of revelation.

"I apologise for yesterday," Adamson said, leaning forward. "Newton told me you were quite upset about the proxy measures."

Bishop smiled dryly, shaking her head as if to brush it off. "Never mind. Unfortunately, it is my duty to follow orders."

The Chief looked content, clearly valuing the mutual respect between them, yet Bishop couldn't ignore the gnawing question that had festered since she'd arrived. "Why is Helix here?"

A brief, somewhat uncomfortable silence followed. Then, with a hint of resignation, Adamson spoke, "I had intended to send you to Hong Kong with Lee. He has extensive experience there and you two would have been a good fit. Unfortunately, he's undergoing psychotherapy at the moment, so I had to find a replacement."

Bishop's stomach tightened. *No.*

"Helix is familiar with China," Adamson explained. "He's fluent in Cantonese and Mandarin and knows Hong Kong's ins and outs. He has connections within the Guoanbu, the triads, and the Russian syndicate in Hong Kong. His extensive network will be invaluable for this mission."

Bishop's voice dropped. "Madam, surely you're not suggesting—"

"I'm sending him with you," Adamson stated firmly, leaving no room for argument.

Bishop sat back, stunned. This was not how she had envisioned her next mission. But she was a professional. No matter how complicated the circumstances, she always found a way through. She'd just need to let go of her grudge and let her new partner get on her good side... right?

2 / ORION

// Angel & Islington //

The night was brisk, and streetlights cast long shadows that danced along the pavement. Bishop adjusted her coat against the chill and paced the street as she approached the Islington townhouse. The security camera was onto her, and as expected, the front door opened before she even had the chance to knock.

"Luna!" A voice boomed cheerfully from the doorway. "Long time no see!"

It was Snatch, aka Robert Church, her good friend and MI6 analyst specialising in East and Southeast Asia. Slightly older than her, he had a distinctive look with his bleached hair and dark under-fade, paired with a sense of style that was impossible to miss.

He wasn't your typical geeky analyst; a true hypebeast at heart, his wardrobe was always stocked with the latest streetwear. Bishop had always noticed how he seemed just as at ease navigating the complexities of international espionage as he was selecting the perfect pair of sneakers.

"It's been ages, Rob," Bishop greeted, her tone warm. She gave him a hug and a light kiss on the cheek. "I hope you haven't started on dinner yet," she grinned and held up a takeaway bag from his favourite kebab place.

Snatch was evidently excited. "Woohoo! You're not trying to bribe me, are you?"

"Well..." Bishop grinned.

They settled in Snatch's home office after dinner. High-end gadgets cluttered the smooth, modern desk, a testament to the seriousness with which he approached his work. It was clear he had invested a lot into this setup; the arrangement was far more advanced than the standard-issue equipment at his MI6 cubicle.

Nibbling on his last chip, Snatch booted up the cloud while Bishop nursed her cup of tea.

"Rolf Alexander Richter, codename Helix," he called.

On the glowing holographic touchscreen, Orion—the SIS AI cloud—displayed Helix's profile in a vivid montage of videos, photographs, and text. The first image was a stark headshot of Helix, his expression inscrutable, followed by a series of clips showing him in various high-stakes operations.

Text overlays detailed extensive training, multilingual skills, and quite an impressive background: He graduated from the German military college and joined Bundeswehr's Special Forces, eventually becoming a captain. In 2026, he was recruited by German intelligence before moving to SIS three years ago.

Bishop's eyes widened as she scanned the wealth of information. "A former German soldier and spy working for the Crown? How did that happen?"

"There was no significant motive," Snatch said, shaking his head. "Many say it's due to his close relationship with Chief Adamson; it seemed that she recruited him personally."

Bishop focused on one particular mission highlighted by Orion. "What's this?" She pressed on the holoscreen to open details of the mission.

"Ah yes, last year, your Chief sent him to Shanghai to uncover evidence of China's atmospheric seeding tests. Despite working under the station chief, Adamson gave him the green light to complete the mission solo, which didn't sit well with some higher-ups at MI6. Even D had to step in."

The mention of Director Lester, the elusive director of the Secret Intelligence Service, piqued Bishop's interest. The incident must have caused quite a stir internally; she could only imagine how it had affected the Chief's relationship with her direct superior. Again her mind raced with implications.

She watched as a candid video played, showing Helix covered in a Bedouin cloak in a war-torn village. This would have been from the same mission that she first met him, near Cairo.

"Snatch, could you send me all this information?" Bishop asked.

Snatch quietly tinkered with some permission settings. "There, you should have access to anything related to Helix in the Orion cloud."

Bishop took out her phone, punched in the codes and verified that she indeed had access. "Thanks, you're the best," she said as she gave him a peck on the cheek.

"Just doing my job," Snatch replied with a smile. "Though you know…" he said, leaning forward slightly and putting on his smoothest move, "I've always been crazy about you."

This was a game they both played, the flirtatious banter between the sharp-witted analyst and the shadowy field agent. It was light and entertaining, yet it always seemed like there might be something more.

Bishop pursed her lips into a coquettish smile.

"I know, Snatch. But remember that intra-departmental relationships are against Crown policy," she chuckled, readying to leave.

He rolled his eyes, unsurprised by her response. She always kept him at arm's length, never letting him get too close. In a way, he almost respected her for it.

"You're such a stickler for rules. Can I at least take you out for dinner?"

Her smile softened. "*I* should be taking you to dinner, Rob. When—*if*—I get back from this mission, okay?"

"Okay," Snatch said. "It's a date."

She gave him a sweet, reassuring smile before heading out into the night.

SIS AI Cloud / ORION

REPORT: HONG KONG STATION STATUS

Security clearance: Level 4

Prepared by: Mansfield Clarke, Head of Hong Kong Station

Date: February 18, 2036

OVERVIEW

The Hong Kong station is grappling with severe operational challenges amid escalating political tensions and upcoming elections.

The volatile political landscape has intensified security risks, further complicating our strategic objectives and operational effectiveness.

STATION STATUS

Operational Capacity: Significantly impaired.

Personnel: The station is critically understaffed. Recent losses of key agents and the increased demand for surveillance have stretched our resources to their limits.

Infrastructure: The primary base remains secure, but the surge in political activity has exposed our secondary safehouses and operational sites to heightened risk.

RECENT INCIDENTS

Agent Casualties: Four field agents have been confirmed killed in action due to a coordinated attack by hostile elements linked to Neo-Soviet agents. Two agents are currently severely injured after a confrontation in Kowloon.

OPERATIONAL IMPACT

Field Operations: Severely restricted. The dual impact of personnel shortages and the increased security measures associated with the elections has necessitated the suspension of several key missions.

Intelligence Flow: Significant delays and gaps in actionable data.

Communications: While secure channels remain intact, enhanced encryption and secure drop points are now mandatory.

IMMEDIATE NEEDS

Reinforcements: Urgent deployment of additional field agents with expertise in counterintelligence, counterterrorism, and political espionage is needed.

Medical Support: Immediate augmentation of medical facilities and personnel.

Intelligence Support: Re-establish secure communication lines with allied networks to recover the intelligence pipeline.

RECOMMENDATIONS

Priority Assignment: Reinforce the station with seasoned agents capable of operating under high-pressure conditions, ensuring continuity and stability in our mission objectives.

End of Report

3 / HARMLESS

// Hong Kong //

The announcement over the PA system crackled to life.

```
British Airways Flight BA516 has just landed. Please proceed to Terminal 2 for immigration processing.
```

The two operatives stepped off the flight from Pattaya, blending into the bustling crowd of Hong Kong International airport. They walked hand in hand, their guise an orchestrated performance. A barrage of screens greeted them as they approached the immigration counter.

The customs officer glanced up from his desk, eyeing the pair. "Welcome to Hong Kong, Mister Mattiassen. Business or pleasure?"

Helix flashed a warm, practised smile, the kind that could disarm even the most sceptical observer. "Oh, definitely pleasure." He turned slightly, lowering his voice just enough that it felt like an intimate secret. "Right, darling?"

Bishop played along, her grip tightening on Helix's arm as she leaned in, her voice dripping with saccharine sweetness. "Yes. But remember, honey, you promised no hustling while on holiday." She added a playful pucker, her lips inches from his cheek.

The officer stamped their passports with a dull thud. "Enjoy your stay."

"Thank you," Bishop chirped, her tone syrupy but sincere. As they moved past the immigration desk, her expression hardened, though she maintained a veneer of casual charm.

"Could you, perhaps, release your grip on my hip?"

Helix arched an eyebrow. He had been patient. Sure, he was not the social type and did not expect to be instant friends with his new partner. But after two flights, countless hours in close proximity, and the ever-present game of barbed remarks, he was getting tired of this.

He slid his hand off her hip with deliberate care. "You should be a bit nicer to your pretend husband. After all, this whole 'intimate newlywed' act was your brilliant idea."

She shot him a withering glare. "Oh please, I would rather not. But this is a much more believable cover than pretending to be consulate envoys."

As professionals, they had meticulously crafted every detail of their new identities—everything from their fabricated family backgrounds and their supposed meet-cute to the number of guests at their imaginary wedding. It could have been a fun exercise, if only her partner wasn't this guy.

Her tone turned thoughtful as she scanned the packed airport, professional instincts taking over. "Orion was right though; a record number of travellers have been coming in and out of Hong Kong and Macau these past few weeks. Very unusual given it's not even high season. I'm getting the vibes of Berlin during the Cold War."

Helix allowed a smirk to play on his lips, "You've been doing some reading."

She took it as an offence. "And why is that such a surprise?"

His gaze turned icy. "Just learn to take a compliment, Bishop."

She responded with an eyeroll, aware of the childishness of her reaction, but unable to suppress the irritation that flared within her. Ever since the start of their mission, the man's detached responses, or lack thereof, felt like a slap in her face. He commanded an air of superiority that grated on her nerves. Every casual glance, every composed response, felt like a challenge, a reminder of the silent rivalry simmering between them.

Setting all that aside, they collected their luggage and stepped into the heart of Hong Kong, straight into the high-stakes game they were about to play.

The MI6 headquarters in Hong Kong was a blend of futuristic technology and a traditional British decor. Clarke, a 60-something man with a stern face, was on a voice call with the British consul general, his voice terse and impatient.

"Don't worry, Sir Paul," Clarke said into the phone. "We'll try to resolve this as quickly as possible. But as you know, we're short on personnel… Alright, thank you, sir."

He hung up, clearly annoyed. His gaze shifted to the two agents sitting across from him. The moment his eyes met Helix's, his face soured.

"Well, well," Clarke muttered, barely containing his displeasure. "You're still alive."

"Sorry to disappoint you, Clarke," Helix responded, a faint edge in his voice.

Clarke's expression was cold. "Of all the Special Ops personnel, why is it always you—"

He caught himself and looked at Bishop, who had been waiting patiently. "Oh, sorry. What's your name, miss?"

"Bishop, sir," she replied smoothly, "also Special Ops."

Clarke's demeanour shifted as he addressed her, shaking her hand. "Mansfield Clarke, Head of Hong Kong Station." He nursed his electronic pipe and activated the holoscreen. "Right. Given the time constraints, let's get started."

A holographic map of China bathed the room in a soft blue light.

"As you've seen in your case files and all over the news," Clarke began, "Jiang's popularity is surging, especially in wealthy coastal areas like Hong Kong. Despite being new to politics, the Chinese Nationalist League chairman has gained a strong following among young voters by supporting the local economy and modern Chinese culture. He's now leading the polls for the upcoming presidential election."

Clarke's expression grew serious. "Unfortunately for the Allies, this is bad news. His nationalist agenda prioritises domestic growth over foreign investments, and many Western enterprises in China and Hong Kong have already gone under."

He continued, "While this situation may be troubling for some Western investors, there could be potential benefits. Jiang has made it clear that Soviet investors will still have a place in his economy. However, Moscow is unlikely to passively watch the collapse of the Red Pact. The Soviets would rather see a moderate candidate like Liu Xinhong in power."

Clarke's gaze shifted between Helix and Bishop. "Coincidentally, while investigating Soviet connections to Liu…"

"Your agents were compromised and killed," Helix interjected.

Clarke nodded, slightly annoyed. "You're always a quick one."

He resumed, "My suspicions are proving to be correct. The key to unravelling this is tracking the Sluzhba agents operating across China and Hong Kong. If we can prove their collusion with Liu, we'll be one step closer to dismantling the Red Pact. And if that's the goal… the means don't matter."

Bishop and Helix exchanged a look. "Understood," she said firmly. "We'll get to work."

The moon hung high above the glittering cityscape, casting an ethereal glow over the consulate for the Union of Neo-Soviet Republics, a fortified building in the heart of Wanchai.

Bishop and Helix perched on the edge of a rooftop two streets away. The roof they occupied, part of an older mid-rise building with weathered brick and rusted air conditioning units, offered a perfect vantage point.

Bishop adjusted her night vision binoculars, scanning the consulate grounds. Helix, crouched low beside her, peered through his own binoculars. This was their second night staking out the consulate, but after spending a week together, things felt different—sharper.

He turned slightly, catching sight of the taut lines of her body, poised for action yet undeniably feminine.

“I think starting tomorrow, we should divide and conquer. It doesn't take two people to do a recon,” he murmured.

Bishop shot him a glance. “Fine by me. You're the one who insisted on tagging along.”

Their conversation was interrupted by a commotion near the consulate gate. A tall, broad-shouldered man with a distinctive presence stepped out of a black sedan. His demeanour was rough, his eyes darting around with a predatory glint as he leered at a young woman exiting the consulate. Both agents immediately recognised the man from their case files—he was one of Kuznetsov's men.

"Target identified… that's Viktor Karamov, right?" Bishop asked.

"Yeah. I did some in-depth research on him the other day. According to the cloud, his blind spot is… women. Seems like our AI overlord was right."

Bishop exhaled through her nose, unimpressed.

Helix chuckled softly; his eyes still trained on Karamov. "You're up, Bishop. Did you bring a change of clothes?"

She rolled her eyes. "I did, but don't expect me to do this often. The sooner we get the intel and wrap this up, the better."

Helix nodded, a smile playing at the corner of his lips as he appreciated her willingness to go along with his plan. "Why don't you get ready? I'll tail him and let you know where to be," he said, fixing his eyes back on the scene below.

As Bishop stood to leave, she took in the way his muscles tensed under his clothes, and the way his jaw clenched ever so slightly when he was focused. He was infuriatingly competent, a blend of raw strength and control that made him hard to ignore.

Neither would admit it aloud, but they were both sizing each other up, testing boundaries, pushing limits. The mission was important, but so was the battle of wills they were quietly waging.

It was Friday night, and the spirits were high at Wanchai's One-Fifth Bar. A DJ in one corner spun classic funk and soul records from the turn of the century, while the parquet-covered dance floor filled with Hong Kong's glitterati. Designer sofas lined the walls, offering a stylish haven for patrons as they drank and mingled.

Helix lounged in a corner, his gaze fixed on the Soviet agent, Karamov, who was sitting by the bar. The task at hand was a rare treat—a chance to observe Hong Kong's beautiful people in their natural habitat. He took a slow sip of his whisky.

A working girl, dressed in a daringly low-cut cocktail dress and black stilettos, approached his table. Her makeup was heavy, but her smile was polished and inviting. She pointed to the empty space beside him on the sofa.

"Is the seat taken?" she asked, raising her voice slightly to be heard over the pulsating music.

Helix studied her for a moment, a grin spreading across his face. "Yes. Sorry. Please don't come back."

The smile faltered on the girl's face. With a huff, she turned on her heel and walked away. "Who would want to anyway??" she hissed under her breath, leaving a faint trail of perfume behind.

Helix watched her retreating form with a smirk, then shifted his attention back to Karamov under the club's haze of strobe lights and pulsating beats.

What's taking her so long?

He glanced at his watch again. When he looked up, Bishop emerged from the ladies' room.

She wore a strapless, knee-length black leather dress that accentuated her curves. A hint of smoke adorned her eyelids, and earrings dangled from her delicate earlobes. She moved through the crowd with practised ease, her every step exuding confidence. Despite himself, Helix raised an eyebrow.

She made her way to the bar, weaving through the throng of club goers, her eyes locked on the target.

"Could I get a Black Russian, please?" she called out to the bartender, her voice cutting through the music.

"Coming right up," the bartender replied.

She slid onto the stool beside Karamov, who immediately turned his head to rove appreciatively over her form. She caught his eye and smiled.

He posed her a question, but with the loudness, she leaned in closer.

"Isn't it a bit late for caffeine?" he repeated, putting on his most charming smile. "Unless you're planning to stay up all night…"

Bishop chuckled softly. She turned her head to study him. He was a few years older than her, with features that marked him as distinctly Russian. She tilted her head, her voice playful. "Unfortunately, my body's immune to coffee," she replied smoothly, "I can barely stay awake without one."

When the bartender delivered her cocktail, Karamov slipped a banknote under his palm, instructing him to keep the change.

"You shouldn't have—" Bishop began.

"Don't mention it," he interrupted, his hand brushing against hers. "You can get the next round."

"In that case..." she lifted her glass in a toast, "cheers."

"Cheers," he echoed, clinking his glass against hers.

Helix observed from his seat, a dry smile on his lips. He finished his drink and ordered another shot from a passing waiter, his gaze never straying far from the unfolding interaction.

Bishop knew the game well. It was a delicate balance of charm and deception, and she played her part with finesse, having honed it through countless hours of training and practice. The bar's pulsating music created a backdrop for their flirtation, which grew more intense as the night wore on.

Every move, every glance, was calculated to draw him in. She leaned closer to Karamov, her perfume mixing with the smoky haze in the air. Her voice was a low, inviting murmur as she spoke, each word carefully chosen to maintain the illusion of genuine interest. As she laughed at his jokes, her eyes sparkled with mischief, and her hand brushed against his arm, lingering just a moment longer than necessary.

Trailing his fingers down her bare shoulders, Karamov whispered: "How about we move somewhere more comfortable?"

Bishop's laughter faded into a sultry smile, her lips curving in a way that promised more than just conversation. "Where do you have in mind?" she asked, her tone smooth and teasing.

They left the bar, and headed toward the coat room to grab her jacket. Helix, still watching from his table, placed a hand over his mouth. He knew the game well, too, but couldn't shake the feeling that everything felt just a little too easy…

The city lights filtered through the window as Karamov led Bishop into his sleek, high-rise apartment just a few buildings from the bar. The space was minimalist yet luxurious, with ambient lighting casting shadows on the walls.

Despite the professionalism and the objective, Bishop could never entirely ignore the discomfort that came with sexual entrapments. She knew that male operatives were subjected to similar training, their charm and allure used as tools just as hers was. It was a necessary part of the job, but it didn't always make it any easier to endure.

She masked her uneasiness with a flirtatious smile as she stepped inside. “Nice place,” she commented, letting her eyes roam around.

“Make yourself at home,” Karamov offered, his voice smooth while gesturing towards the plush sofa. “Would you like a drink?”

“No thank you, I've had plenty already…”

Her eyes were alert, her senses sharp despite the light-headedness from all the vodka she'd downed. When he moved closer to her and began feeling her up, she pushed back slightly.

She needed to buy time to gauge his knowledge. “How about we move to the bedroom? It's a bit cramped here...”

But his eyes darkened with intent as he pushed her down onto the sofa, his lips trailing hungrily down her neck and collarbone with a touch of roughness—not the kind of prelude she was expecting.

She noticed the way his hand brushed against his jean pocket in an oddly purposeful manner. Her instincts flared as she caught a glint of metal in the dim light.

In one decisive move, she landed a sharp kick to his stomach, sending him stumbling backward. The gun tumbled from his pocket and skidded across the floor.

They both lunged for the weapon. Karamov managed to strike her in the rib, the impact knocking the wind out of her and doubling her over.

He grabbed for the gun, but her recovery was swift as she threw a powerful side kick into his ribs that sent him crashing into a nearby table.

Bishop finally reached the gun, her fingers closing around the handle just as Karamov lunged at her again with a mix of shock and pain on his face.

Without a second thought, she pulled the trigger. The sharp crack of the gunshot echoed through the room as he crumpled to the floor, a bullet nested between his brows, his eyes wide with disbelief.

She stood over him, her face a mask of steely resolve that concealed some of the adrenaline running through her. The sudden rustling behind her made her snap the gun back into position, the cold steel aimed squarely at the intruder.

"It's me," came the urgent whisper.

Helix stepped into view, taking in the scene with a cold, professional gaze. "Not bad," he remarked while glancing at Karamov's lifeless body.

Bishop barely acknowledged him, instead she smoothed her dishevelled hair and adjusted her dress, trying to regain some semblance of normalcy.

"Are you okay?" His voice softened as he observed her.

Her response was clipped. "Yeah. Just a little bloated." She reached into her purse and pulled out a pair of gloves.

"No surprise there," he murmured, "you were drinking like a camel."

She shot him a glare but didn't say anything.

Helix tightened his gloves. "Anyway, let's get moving. We don't have much time."

Moments later, two Neo-Soviet operatives stormed into the apartment: a woman with a spiky red bob, and a stocky Chinese man with shoulder-length black hair.

They quickly assessed the scene: the lifeless body sprawled on the floor, and the place having been ransacked with paperwork and other paraphernalia scattered across the rooms.

Vareleva, with a grim smirk, turned to Zhao, her underling.

"Doesn't look good, does it?"

They moved to a corner where a hidden camera had been set up. Zhao replayed the footage on his tablet, his eyes narrowing as he saw Bishop's decisive action and Karamov being killed with his own gun.

"Who sent her?" He asked.

"British intelligence," replied Vareleva.

Zhao raised an eyebrow. "You know her?"

Vareleva scrutinised the video. "That girl is part of MI6's Special Ops Division. She's a British national with Malaysian-Chinese roots, who served in the army before joining the UK's Special Forces. She's got top-notch credentials: field operations, counter-terrorism, and assassinations. For the past year, she's been living in Moscow, systematically taking out Soviet military leaders, one by one."

She scoffed, the corners of her mouth curling. "Looks like I've found a worthy opponent, Zhao."

Zhao rolled his eyes; he was used to his team leader's narcissism by now.

"The fact that they're deploying their special unit now..." Vareleva continued, "it's clear MI6 is running out of options."

Zhao nodded, his attention shifting to the figure of Helix entering the scene. "What about the man? He looks familiar."

Vareleva shook her head, half-laughing. "You don't need to worry about him. He's harmless. Kuznetsov himself vouched for him."

She went back to the living room and scanned Karamov's body, sending a short text to call in the agency's cleaners. Then she said, in Russian:

"What a shame, Viktor. Kuznetsov did warn us about this girl and her pretend friend."

Turning on her heel, she added: "You should have listened, comrade."

In the MI6 safehouse, a two-bed apartment in a high-rise on Connaught Road, Helix sat in the dark study, his eyes glued to the tablet screen in front of him.

He watched the recording from the bug he'd left in Karamov's apartment. The sound of Vareleva and Zhao's voices came through his earbuds.

Helix paused the recording and rewound it, playing Vareleva's words again.

"*You don't need to worry about him. He's harmless. Kuznetsov himself vouched for him.*"

A flicker of irritation crossed his face as he replayed the segment once more.

"*You don't need to worry about him. He's harmless. Kuznetsov himself vouched for him.*"

His jaw tightened. He couldn't afford to misstep, not now. The wheels in his mind were turning, wondering what his next move should be.

4 / THE CHASE

Helix jogged along the winding trails near the apartment, the rhythmic thud of his sneakers against the pavement a comforting constant.

This was a city that he knew well yet one that never ceased to amaze him. The modern glass façades of high-rise buildings contrasted sharply with the vibrant, colourful stalls lining the streets below, where vendors hawked everything from steaming bowls of congee to sex toys to bootleg electronics.

When he returned from his morning jog, sweat was glistening on his forehead. He nodded at the building concierge, who greeted him with a polite smile, then headed to the elevator to punch in Floor 32.

"Oh, you're back," Bishop called out as he entered their suite. She was in the study, speaking with Clarke, whose face filled the holoscreen in high definition, wrinkles and all.

"We've got back one of the files that we found at Karamov's place," she said.

Helix joined her, glancing at the decrypted data displayed on the screen. "Isn't this just a list of Soviet companies based in Hong Kong?"

"Correct," Clarke confirmed. "More precisely, these are all companies owned by conglomerate Grigory Safin, who has ties with the Cheyevskaya Group's Hong Kong branch."

Bishop furrowed her brow at the mention of the Russian syndicate. "Are they front companies for the mafia?"

Helix shook his head. "Even if they are, I doubt this has anything to do with our mission. From what I know, the boss of Cheyevskaya HK, a man they call Levski, is very anti-Soviet government. He's had more than a few run-ins with Sluzhba agents in the past."

Clarke's eyes narrowed slightly. "Since you seem to know a lot about this, how about you investigate further?"

Helix maintained a calm demeanour. "Sorry, Clarke, but Bishop and I are already handling quite a few tasks."

Clarke's tone grew more authoritative. "If casualties continue to mount on our side, your workload will only increase, Helix."

Helix countered, "I just think there's no connection between the Russian mafia and the deaths of your agents—"

"When did you switch careers to become an analyst?" Clarke cut him off.

Bishop stepped in, trying to calm the hostility. "Gentlemen, please. Clarke, to be fair, we weren't briefed about this by Chief Adamson—"

An official letter with Chief Adamson's seal suddenly appeared on screen.

Clarke's expression was smug. "Your Chief has given her approval. If you have time to argue, might as well use it for something more productive."

With that, he signed off. Bishop stared at the screen, her exasperation evident as she rubbed her temples.

"Told you," Helix muttered. "Sweet talk is pointless with him."

"Don't be so dismissive," Bishop said. "What do we do now?"

Helix pulled out his phone. "Time to contact an old friend. Do you like pho?"

That evening, they pulled up to a fusion Vietnamese restaurant in Hong Kong's latest up-and-coming district. The place buzzed with energy, a seamless blend of traditional charm and modern flair. As they entered,

Helix immediately spotted his old friend, the owner of the restaurant.

"Sylvia," Helix called out, a broad smile lighting up his face.

"Alex!" She exclaimed, her voice filled with excitement as she approached them.

"Hi, Sylvia," Helix said, admiring her. "You look beautiful as ever. Sorry for the sudden call," he added.

Sylvia waved off his apology. "No problem at all." She was a stunning svelte figure with striking blond ringlets. Her Russian accent added a layer of intrigue to her captivating presence. She turned to Bishop, curiosity in her eyes.

Helix began: "Oh, Syl, let me introduce you to my friend…"

Bishop said, coolly, "Just call me 'Charlie'."

"Nice to meet you, Charlie." Sylvia extended her hand.

Bishop shook her hand. "Likewise."

As they settled at the table and the bowls of steaming pho arrived, Sylvia's gaze settled on Bishop, who hardly touched her food. Despite the uncertainty of what they were doing here, she remained composed, her face giving nothing away.

Sylvia decided to break the silence. "Anyway, Alex, I didn't realise you knew Safin."

Helix took a sip of his tea before responding. "Oh, I don't know him that well. We just played mahjong once, in Shanghai."

His cover at the time had been that of an insurance magnate's heir, and Safin had really taken a liking to him. Though he wasn't above being a honeypot when the mission called for it, he was kind of relieved that the older man was too decent to go through with it.

"Why the sudden interest in Safin now?" Sylvia asked.

Helix leaned in slightly, his tone serious. "Recently, we intercepted a secret document from a local Soviet agent. Upon further investigation, the document contained a list of all Safin's companies with ties to the Cheyevskaya Group... strange, isn't it?"

Sylvia paused, her chopsticks hovering over her bowl. "Are you saying the corrupt officials in Moscow are spying on us?"

Helix shook his head. "Not exactly. I actually thought you might be working *with* them..."

Sylvia chuckled softly, but her eyes were sharp. "Oh, that's definitely not possible. Levski hates dealing with government agents, and Safin respects that."

Helix pressed on. "So, are they really spying on you?"

Sylvia's expression shifted slightly, but she deflected. "Don't jump to conclusions, Alex. Where exactly did you get this information?"

Helix pulled out his phone and showed her a picture of Karamov. "This man... was one of our targets. He was suspected of being involved in the murder of several British agents recently. We found a lot of interesting data at his place. It seems he was working under Kuznetsov, the head of the Soviet station in Hong Kong, tasked with spying on suspicious UNSR citizens."

Sylvia studied Karamov's picture intently. "Hmm... I'll ask Nicolai to investigate."

Helix nodded appreciatively. "We would be very grateful."

Bishop finally chimed in, her voice cutting through the sense of dread. "Um, may I ask something?"

Sylvia turned to her, a polite smile on her lips. "Of course."

"How's business these days, amidst all the election furor?" Bishop inquired, with keen eyes.

"Business is going well. Sure, many Soviet businesses have recently left China, but Cheyevskaya Group is known for its resilience against nationalist waves. In times like these, we must cleverly utilise our extensive and trustworthy local connections."

Bishop pressed on. "Extensive and trustworthy local connections... Do you mean the triads?"

Sylvia's eyes sharpened as she studied the pair before her. Helix pondered aloud, "Good point. The last I heard about Safin, he was busy setting up a luxury casino with the Zong Triad."

Sylvia smiled. "You must mean 'Casinopolis' on Lantau Island. It's indeed a place where Chinese tycoons and Russian mafia bosses go to make friends."

Helix and Bishop exchanged a significant glance. They were onto something.

Helix quipped, "Looks like I need to sharpen up my card skills."

The streets were a blur of neon lights as they cruised through the city, their black sedan blending seamlessly with the evening traffic. Helix was driving, and Bishop was deep in thought.

"Helix..." she broke the silence.

He responded with a simple "Hm?" without taking his eyes off the road.

"Is Sylvia working for us?" she asked, her tone cautious.

He let out a short laugh. "As if she would. Her husband, Nicolai, is Levski's prized protégé. That alone guarantees them a comfortable life, don't you think?"

She frowned, pressing further. "So why would she help a foreign spy like you?"

He shrugged, the corners of his mouth curling into a small, knowing smile. "Well, let's just say we have a mutually beneficial arrangement."

Suspicion crept into her voice. "But isn't it risky to reveal our mission details to a mafia princess?"

She wondered briefly if the arrangement he spoke of was more than just business. Was there something romantic? Sexual? The thought unsettled her, though she wasn't sure why.

"Relax," he replied, his tone nonchalant. "Sylvia can be trusted."

"Where and how did you even meet her?" she asked again, not satisfied with the answer.

"An old friend introduced us—" Helix began, but cut himself off. He ran a hand through his hair, his patience wearing thin. "Enough with the interrogation, it's getting hot in here. Or... are you jealous?"

Bishop rolled her eyes, dismissing the comment, but before she could respond, her gaze shifted to the rear-view mirror, catching sight of a car trailing them. "Speaking of which, that SUV behind us..."

He interrupted, "It's been following us since two traffic lights ago."

"Is the rear camera still working?" she asked, connecting her phone to the car's computer. The sedan was pretty basic—no luxury features, just the essentials. Though decently maintained, she knew it was a product of budget cuts.

On the contrary, behind them, the SUV was a beast on wheels, with a reinforced suspension that absorbed every bump and turn. The windows were heavily tinted, but not the front windshield. Bishop zoomed in closer and instantly clocked the occupant in the backseat.

"I recognise this woman from our case files... she's Kuznetsov's right-hand agent—"

"Evgena Bairamova, codename Vareleva," Helix finished her sentence.

Now fully aware of their pursuers, he made a quick decision. He pressed down on the accelerator, weaving the car through the traffic as he made a sharp turn toward a narrow alley.

But the SUV behind them also picked up speed, its headlights glaring through the rear window as Vareleva and her men closed the gap. Helix took another sharp turn, barrelling down a ramp into the entrance of the cross-harbour tunnel.

"Err, where are you taking us?" she asked.

His eyes were steely, his mind concentrating on the task at hand. "The usual tactics won't work against them. I'm going to try and trap them in the markets of Kowloon... And I need you to be the 'eyeball'."

She shot him an incredulous look. "Are you sure that's a good idea—"

"Just do it, Bishop!" Helix snapped, his voice urgent as they sped into the tunnel, their pursuers hot on their tail.

The roar of engines filled the tunnel as the SUV followed them in, its turbocharged engine growling as it kept a relentless pace.

Helix kept his focus on the road ahead, his hands steady on the wheel as he pushed the car to its limits. They burst out of the tunnel and Bishop warned him of the approaching SUV from their five o'clock.

"Hold on tight!" He shouted, accelerating through the narrow, hectic streets of Kowloon, the night market sprawled out before them in a cacophony of lights, colours, and people.

"Watch out!" Bishop yelled as Helix narrowly avoided a collision with a vendor's cart. Chaos erupted as pedestrians scrambled to get out of the way. The SUV was still on their tail, its engine roaring as it closed the distance, smashing through stalls and sending a shower of debris into the air.

"They're still following us!" Bishop's voice was tense. "We can't keep this up!"

Helix saw the dead end approaching and made a snap decision. He threw the car into reverse, the sudden change in direction causing Bishop to grip the door handle tightly. "What are you doing?" she demanded, eyes wide as the sedan hurtled backward toward the SUV.

Inside the SUV, Vareleva urged her driver to speed up. "Faster! We can't let them get away!" But as she saw the sedan's reverse lights blazing, she saw the strategic shift in their plan. "Reverse! Reverse!" she shouted, looking back to make sure the path was clear.

But it was too late. As the distance between the vehicles closed, Helix shouted, "Duck, Bishop!" and sharply turned the wheel. The side of the sedan screeched against the SUV as they passed, crumpling the door and shearing off the rearview mirror on Bishop's side of the car.

Despite the impact, she saw a split-second chance. She unclipped her seatbelt and reached for her sidearm, rolling down her window. Just as she lined up a shot, Helix abruptly spun the car around, throwing her sideways and slamming her hard into his side with the force of the turn.

Anger flared in her eyes, but before she could react, he stomped on the accelerator, sending the sedan hurtling into a narrow alley. The force of the speed pinned her against the central console, but the urgency of the chase left no room for argument.

Up ahead, the street narrowed into an even tighter alley, barely wide enough for their car. Helix didn't hesitate, plowing forward at full speed.

The SUV, which by then had also done a 360-degree turn, attempted to follow, but the alley was too narrow. The vehicle scraped against the brick walls on both sides, sparks flying as metal met stone, before coming to a screeching halt, wedged in place.

Vareleva, seething with frustration, slinked out of an open window and stormed out. She approached the sedan on foot, gun drawn, but it was already empty, its doors flung open.

She slammed the door with a forceful kick, her fury boiling over and her eyes blazing with fury. "Damn it!" she hissed, her voice a low, venomous growl. "I'll kill them!"

The car chase had been a disaster, forcing the two operatives to escape on foot and by transit. Now back at the safehouse, they were both out of breath and the night's stifling humidity did not help their cause.

Bishop stormed across the dimly lit room, her movements sharp, agitated. She was still running hot—from the chase, from frustration, and from the man currently ignoring her.

"Helix!"

No response. She turned, stepping into his path, blocking his way with a forceful presence.

"Helix! Are you even listening? We need to talk!"

He barely looked at her as he brushed past. "Can we talk later? I need a shower."

"No!" Her voice was sharper than intended. "I need to know what you were thinking back there!"

He sighed deeply, running a hand through his damp, tousled hair.

She planted both hands on her hips. "It's already bad enough we had to ditch the car. Why didn't you let me take the shot?"

His lips curled into a sardonic smile. "You think your sidearm could have penetrated an armoured vehicle?"

Her eyes flashed with anger. "I was aiming for the wheels."

"Enough, Bishop," he said, his voice dropping to a low, dangerous growl. "Against a faster, stronger vehicle, we were lucky to escape at all. We can discuss this later."

"No," she snapped, stepping closer. "What do I write in my report? Losing both the target *and* the car? Unlike you, I'm not the Chief's fav—" she stopped herself, but it was too late.

"The Chief's favourite, you mean?" His expression darkened. "I'm disappointed, Bishop. I thought you were above petty gossip."

The words were barely out of his mouth when she summoned all her strength and connected her fist with his jaw, sharp and satisfying. The force of the punch sent him staggering back, blood trickling from the corner of his lips. He touched his bleeding mouth, his gaze shifting to meet hers with a mix of surprise and something darker.

"I've been wanting to do that for a long time," she shouted. "Now come on!"

Despite her tense anticipation, he remained still. Brushing the blood from his lips, he stated: "I'm not going to fight you. Don't make me."

That only made her want to hit him again.

She threw another punch, but he was ready. He caught her arm in a firm grip. "Enough!" he commanded, his voice carrying an underlying heat.

Ignoring his command, she swung her other fist toward his ribs, but he deflected the blow with his forearm. Undeterred, she brought her knee up toward his groin in a vicious arc. He anticipated the move, shifting his weight to the side just in time to avoid the strike, and in a fluid motion, he stepped forward, closing the distance between them.

She twisted in his grasp, trying to free herself, but he was relentless. She swung again, this time aiming for his face, but he blocked it effortlessly, his hand capturing her wrist. The next moment, he spun her around, pressing her back against his chest, her arms twisted painfully behind her.

"I said enough!" he growled.

She gritted her teeth, straining against his hold. She could feel the raw power in his tense muscles, coiled and ready, just as controlled as the anger simmering in his voice.

"Listen, Bishop! I didn't come all the way here to babysit you. From now on, we have to learn to talk and behave like two mature adults, is that understood?"

When she answered with more struggles and ragged gasps, he repeated his query. "Is that understood??" he demanded, his breath hot against her face.

"Yes, yes!" she finally shouted. "Let me off!"

He loosened his hold and she immediately sprang away, stopping only when his voice cut through the air again.

"I don't know why the Chief sent us both to Hong Kong..." he muttered under his breath.

She spun around. "I should be the one saying that! She must be having a laugh! You, of all people... Try putting yourself in my shoes, Helix! I spent a year in Moscow—"

"Don't tell me you're still bitter about the last mission," he interrupted.

"A year in that darned place!" Her voice pierced through the walls and his eardrums. "Do you know how many I had to kill to get close to Zaitsev, and just as I was about to finish it, they sent a proxy to take out my target?" She staggered back. "You know what? Forget it! A first-rate agent like you will never understand."

Helix watched in silence as she slumped against the wall and then sank to the floor in frustration and fatigue. This mission had become a labyrinth of danger and deception that they would have to navigate together, whether they liked it or not. So they had better learn to get along.

He stood and walked over to her.

"Hey," he said, his voice suddenly gentle, "as I said time and time again, I only came to Moscow under orders. But if this makes you feel better… then I'm sorry."

He settled beside her on the floor, the closeness shifting the dynamic between them. Her eyes, usually so guarded, met his. "I respect that. Sorry for hitting you."

A playful smile tugged at his lips. "It's fine. Didn't really hurt."

Her growl made him chuckle, the laughter easing the tension.

"You're quite the ruthless killer, aren't you?" He noted.

"Once upon a time," she replied, her voice tinged with melancholy, "I used to dream about the faces of those I'd killed. But the dead stopped talking, and the person I was never came back."

His gaze lingered on her face, tracing the curve of her lips and the remaining flush of emotion that coloured her cheeks. The intensity in her eyes, now softened by the weight of their discussion, stirred something within him.

"Luna," he said softly as he stood up.

She raised an eyebrow, intrigued.

"That's your real name, isn't it?" He smiled, walking to the door. "Don't take this the wrong way, Luna, but you remind me of myself when I was younger."

"Helix!" she snapped, putting her hands back on her waist. "Can you stop being so bloody patronising for once!"

Her reaction amused him to no end. "Alright, alright, I promise," he said with a smirk, and approached the door that led to the apartment corridor.

"But in return, please call me 'Alex'." His voice was softer now, his request personal.

With that, he unlocked the door, and stepped inside.

5 / ENTANGLEMENT

SIS AI Cloud / ORION
SUBJECT REPORT: Potential Dynamic Between Operatives 'Helix' and 'Bishop'

Security clearance: Level 7
Commissioned by: Leonor Adamson, Chief of Special Operations
Report date: March 11, 2036

OVERVIEW

'Helix' and 'Bishop' are both operatives in the Special Operations Division. The analysis considers their individual profiles, operational histories, and potential areas of synergy or conflict during joint missions. Additionally, this report explores the likelihood of romantic entanglement between the two operatives.

AGENT PROFILES

Helix

- Strengths: Highly adaptable, resourceful, and capable of thinking outside the box. Exhibits strong strategic acumen and is effective in complex, fluctuating situations.
- Concerns: Tendency to challenge authority and deviate from established protocols when he believes it necessary for mission success.

Bishop

- Strengths: Disciplined, reliable. Demonstrates a strong respect for the chain of command and is effective in structured operations.
- Concerns: May exhibit rigidity in fast-changing scenarios, with a preference for procedure over improvisation.

DYNAMIC ANALYSIS

Complementary Strengths

Helix's ability to think on his feet can fill gaps when rigid plans fail, while Bishop's methodical approach ensures that operations stay on course. Together, they have the potential to cover a wide range of operational needs.

Potential for Dispute

In situations where rapid decisions are necessary, Helix might act independently, which could cause friction.

Operational Synergy

Despite the potential for dispute, if effectively managed, their contrasting approaches could result in highly effective teamwork.

POTENTIAL ENTANGLEMENT

Compatibility Indicators

- Age & Experience: Both operatives are within a close age range, suggesting they may relate well on a generational level. Their similar field experience could foster mutual respect and understanding.
- Contrasting Personalities: Their dynamic may lead to 'yin-yang' attraction, where each finds in the

other qualities they may lack or admire.
- Physical Attributes: Both operatives possess strong attributes often associated with traditional attractiveness, increasing the likelihood of mutual attraction.

Concerns and Risks

- Professional Boundaries: A romantic relationship could complicate interactions, particularly in high-stress or high-risk situations where emotional decisions might compromise mission integrity.
- Conflict of Interest: If a romantic relationship were to develop, it could lead to partiality in decision-making.
- Emotional Impact: The high-risk nature of their work could intensify emotional connections, potentially leading to distractions or disagreements that impact their effectiveness in the field.

CONCLUSION

The dynamic between Helix and Bishop presents both opportunities and challenges, and romantic entanglement could complicate their operational effectiveness. Careful monitoring and clear boundary setting are recommended to ensure mission success and maintain professional integrity.

RECOMMENDATIONS

- Consider joint training exercises to improve communication and mutual understanding.
- Monitor their interactions for any signs of romantic entanglement and address potential issues early.
- Establish clear operational roles and responsibilities before missions.
- Implement protocols to manage potential conflicts of interest if a relationship develops.

End of Report
ORION / Eyes in the Shadows

The fist fight did wonders to alleviate the friction between them, and gradually, Bishop and Helix found a new rhythm in their partnership. Without the constant friction of their earlier clashes, their combined skills shone brightly. His keen instincts and her precise, methodical approach allowed them to set up an effective network of local assets and surveillance to monitor the movements of Cheyevskaya and the Zong Triad; this on top of their original mission objective of finding proof that the Soviets were aiding Jiang Yaozu's rival.

Though Bishop was reluctant to admit it, she could see why Helix was—allegedly—Chief Adamson's favourite. He had been in intelligence twice as long as she had, and the experience showed. The fact that he had built a formidable reputation within German and British agencies, and his ability to operate in multiple Asian theatres with fluency and cultural ease, was also intriguing to her.

She had never been the type to be easily swayed by appearances, but something about him had captured her attention from the moment they met. It was less about his good looks and more in the way he carried himself: calm, confident and always in control, as if the world couldn't touch him.

From Helix's part, he was also beginning to respect what the Chief saw in Bishop. She was relatively young, but there was no denying her tenacity, intuition, and adaptability. Her allure was less about a single feature and more about the entire package—she was fierce, but there was also a natural elegance in the way she held herself.

They had recently established a thrice-weekly routine to keep fit at the apartment gym, doing cardio and spotting each other when lifting weights. This was their first sparring exercise.

They stood facing each other on the mat, both in workout gear. They began by circling each other, sizing up the other, moving with the smoothness of seasoned fighters.

Bishop wasn't exceptionally strong, but had honed her skills through a mix of disciplines. From a young age, she learned Wing Chun from her British-Chinese father. As a teenager, she spent time street fighting with local young thugs. Later, her training expanded to include boxing and Muay Thai, reflecting the preferences of the British armed forces.

She struck first, a swift jab aimed at his face. He dodged it smoothly, countering with a low kick that she blocked with her knee. She responded with a flurry of punches, which he blocked and parried, his own strikes interspersed with quick attempts at grappling her into submission.

He managed to catch her arm, attempting to use a wrestling technique to bring her down. She, however, twisted her body with remarkable agility, breaking free and using his momentum against him to flip him onto the mat.

He landed with a grunt but quickly rolled back to his feet, a grin spreading across his face. "Nice one."

She didn't let up, pressing her advantage with a series of calculated kicks and strikes. He blocked most of them but took a few hits, appreciating her skill more and more. He countered with a Krav Maga move, aiming to disarm her, but she slipped out of his grasp, fluid as water.

They clashed again, this time him using his grappling skills to try and pin her, his strength and technique on full display. Their bodies became a blur of motion, each trying to gain the upper hand. Finally, with a swift move, he locked her onto the mat, their faces inches apart. His breath was ragged, his muscles straining to keep her down.

Bishop's eyes were filled with defiance and just a hint of respect for his finesse. She conceded. "You win this round."

Helix released her and stood up. He offered her a hand, which she took, pulling herself up. "You're a tough opponent, Luna." *Despite your petite size,* he silently observed.

She took a moment to regroup, mentally replaying the spar and noting his fighting technique. "You've got some very effective moves yourself," she said thoughtfully, “but next time, I’ll be the one pinning you to the floor.”

She realised her poor choice of words when he snickered.

“You know what I mean,” she quickly added, slightly embarrassed.

“Yep,” he replied with a glint in his eye. “We’ll see who gets to be on top next time.”

She couldn’t ignore the double entendres, nor the blatant flirtatiousness that had seeped into their every exchange, one that danced on the edge of propriety. Any other man, and she might’ve dismissed it as inappropriate. But this was Helix, and that made it complicated.

Shaking her head, she mentally refocused and continued her workout. Work was her priority, and she needed to channel her energy into the mission, not get tangled up in forbidden attractions.

The modern art gallery perched high in the Mid-Levels, offering a panoramic view of the shimmering skyline. Inside, a crowd of elites moved gracefully between minimalist sculptures and oversized canvases. The air was filled with the muted murmur of conversations and the occasional clink of glasses.

They made their entrance, perfectly attuned to their surroundings: Helix in a tailored suit with a crisp white shirt, hair slicked back, and Bishop in a form-fitting burgundy cocktail dress. They wore fibre-optic glasses equipped with embedded cameras, designed to scan and cross-reference the gallery's attendees with the Orion database.

Their primary objective was to observe, record, and identify key players potentially linked to the Cheyevskaya and Zong Triad. Their secondary goal was to gather evidence that these groups were using hybrid art pieces—both physical artworks and digital NFTs—to launder money.

Helix manoeuvred through the gallery with ease, his touch light but deliberate on Bishop's lower back. "You've got that 'art curator' look down perfectly," he whispered, his tone teasing. Bishop smiled, her eyes scanning the room as they approached a large abstract painting: a swirl of reds and blacks that seemed to pulse with energy.

While Bishop appeared absorbed in the artwork, her glasses discreetly recorded the faces and movements of those around them. The gallery buzzed with the presence of tycoons, socialites, and individuals whose wealth and influence often hid darker dealings. As they navigated the crowd, her gaze fell on a group of men near a sculpture. Their body language hinted at shared secrets, and she adjusted her glasses to capture their images.

Helix leaned in closer, his lips brushing against her temple as he murmured, "Left corner. The tall one in the grey suit. He's Cheyevskaya." Her heart rate quickened with their closeness, but her eyes followed his indication. The man was conversing with a Chinese individual wearing a jade ring—a clear marker of significance within the Zong Triad.

As they continued to circulate, they moved in sync, as if they had done this a thousand times before. In a secluded alcove, they encountered a painting that starkly contrasted the rest of the gallery—a dreamlike landscape bathed in soft, otherworldly light.

Bishop stopped, genuinely captivated by the piece. Helix paused beside her. For a brief moment, their operation seemed to fade into the background as they stood side by side, absorbing the artwork's ethereal beauty. He caught a glimpse of her form, the delicate lighting accentuating the softness of her Eurasian features.

The moment passed, and they recentred on their mission, but the connection lingered.

They finished their sweep of the gallery. At the exit, he glanced at her, a small, almost imperceptible smile on his lips.

"Since we're both dressed up, how about dinner at Le Mirage?" he suggested casually.

Bishop raised a brow at the mention of the Michelin-starred rooftop restaurant overlooking the harbour.

"Don't we need a reservation?" she asked.

Helix grinned. "Surely you can come up with a good cover to get us in without one?" he challenged.

She tilted her head and chuckled, a plan already forming in her mind. "OK, but only if you're paying."

He offered his arm with a playful smile. She looked at him and took it, playing along and secretly enjoying the gesture.

The Port of Hong Kong buzzed with activity under the cloak of night. Cranes towered like mechanical giants, their silhouettes stark against the illuminated cityscape. Containers stacked high formed a labyrinth, and the constant drone of machinery filled the air.

Bishop and Helix, clad in reflective vests and hard hats, moved among the longshoremen. Falsified credentials had granted them access, but the real challenge lay ahead. They were chasing another lead, evidence that Safin's connection to the Zong Triad could be found among these imported—or more likely smuggled—goods.

Setting up behind a container, they removed their disguises, revealing tactical gear underneath. Bishop released three small, silent drones into the air. Each was equipped with thermal imaging capabilities, mapping out the dock and tracking the movement of contraband. Everything was shown through her glasses.

"Over there," she pointed to a group of containers marked with a discreet, almost invisible insignia. "Those look to be Safin's."

They navigated the maze of containers, the drone feed guiding their steps. As they approached Safin's containers, voices drifted over from the other side. Triad members were discussing a new shipment of high-tech weaponry set to be moved through Safin's warehouses.

The drones helped them eavesdrop on the conversation. "They're exchanging money and documents," she whispered, zooming in on the paper trails.

Helix gave her a victorious smile. "Great, now we have solid evidence."

Suddenly, he held up a hand, signalling for her to take cover. They pressed close to a stack of crates, the narrow space forcing them together. A triad member passed by, oblivious to their presence.

Through her glasses, against the holographic display from the drones, Bishop found her gaze settling on Helix's profile, drawn to the subtle details that made him all too human. The slight upturn of his nose lent a boyish charm to his otherwise chiselled features. His soft stubble, evidence of a morning shave forgotten, added a certain ruggedness to him.

"Do we have everything we need?" he asked, pulling back just a tad reluctantly after the coast was clear.

She looked at the data procured by the drones and nodded, sending a command for the drones to return.

A small crash echoed through the container yard. One of the drones had been spotted—and subsequently gunned down. "Drone down," Bishop muttered, activating its kill switch. "I've diverted the other two."

Triad members began to chatter, signalling each other to hunt for the intruder in their midst. Helix acted quickly, deploying a small EMP device that temporarily disabled all nearby electronic devices, security cameras included.

He grabbed Bishop's arm and pulled her along. "Let's go!"

Bullets flew past them, pinging off the metal. Helix created diversions by crashing objects into a stack of crates elsewhere, drawing the guards away from their path. They manoeuvred through the container yard, using hand signals and brief verbal cues to communicate, making their way towards the exit—but found that it was completely blocked.

"Get to the water," Bishop ordered, glancing from the corner of the eye that two armed guards were in their path.

"OK, cover me!" Helix shouted, moving to flank and ambush the triad members.

A shootout erupted. Bishop provided suppressive fire, her aim precise and controlled as she gunned down the two men. They ran, hearts pounding, but there was an undeniable exhilaration in their escape.

He reached the edge of the port first, spotting several boats docked at the pier. Quickly assessing his options, he chose an older, simpler vessel that looked easiest to hotwire. He crouched beside the boat's control panel, prying it open, his fingers deftly working the cables to bypass the ignition while Bishop again provided cover, shooting at their pursuers.

Sparks flew briefly, and the engine roared to life. Bishop leaped in, bullets whizzing past her, striking the wooden dock and sending splinters flying.

Helix steered them away from the dock at high speed. The sound of the engine drowned out the gunfire, but Bishop's sharp eyes caught a glimpse of him wincing as he leaned forward. She quickly moved to check on him, spotting a bullet lodged in the liquid armour on his back.

"I'm fine," he assured her.

As the boat sped away into the night, the lights of the city gradually faded, leaving them in the dark waters, their only companions the sounds of the waves.

Back at the safehouse, Bishop had managed to retrieve the other two drones and, after checking that everything was intact, set them on the dining table. The adrenaline was still pumping through her veins. Her next order of business was to check on her partner.

"Helix, let me take a look," she softly commanded.

He hesitated for a moment before relenting. She guided him to a dining chair and helped him peel off his gear. The liquid armour he wore was impressive, a shiny, dark material that had hardened on impact, but when she lifted his compression top, a dark bruise was already spreading across the point of impact on his upper back.

"I've never liked these experimental materials," she said, almost to herself. "I'll get the healing gel."

She went to fetch a first aid kit from a nearby cabinet and knelt behind him, helping him take off his compression top and removing her own armour. As she worked the cooling gel, she couldn't help but notice the contours of his muscles and the faint scars decorating his back.

He felt the hairs on his neck rise, from the feel of air conditioning on his bare skin, the effect of the gel, and her touch.

"Does it hurt?" she asked.

"A little bit," he admitted, his voice a mix of pain and amusement. "Guess I'm not as invincible as I pretend to be."

She smiled as she applied more of the gel, rubbing it deeply against the sore blue spots across his muscular back, then tapped him gently on the shoulder. "All done," she said softly, but neither of them moved.

He turned around, his eyes searching hers, with a look that made her heart skip a beat. "Thanks."

She felt heat rising and colouring her neck and cheeks. "Are you hit anywhere else?" she asked, trying to steer the conversation away from his dangerous aura.

As she turned away to tidy up the first aid kit, he didn't know if it was her scent, the way her hair was tucked behind her ear, or the curve of her neck that made him tingle. There was something intoxicating about her blend of strength and femininity, even when he knew he should keep his distance.

He reached out slowly, his fingers brushing her jaw, before cupping her face. With a deliberate slowness, he closed the distance between them, capturing her lips in a kiss that was tender but smouldering with unspoken heat. The smell of him—fresh, masculine, with a hint of the adrenaline from their earlier mission—flooded her senses.

For a moment, she froze. But it wasn't long before her body responded, melting into him as her hands gripped the cooling tube she'd been holding, forgotten in the haze of his closeness.

She kissed him back, her lips parting as she carefully explored the depths of his mouth. His hands gripped her waist with a firm insistence, pulling her body tightly against his. In one fluid motion, he stood, lifting her effortlessly onto the table, the cool surface pressing against her thighs as he stepped between her legs.

"Alex—" she managed a weak protest.

But he was already on top of her, his breath hot against her skin. Their lips crashed together again, the kiss now raw and intense, fuelled by the pent-up desire and emotions that had been compounding beneath the surface.

She couldn't hold back anymore. The tube clattered to the floor as her hands threaded into his hair, pulling him closer, deepening the kiss until it was almost frantic, her need for him boiling over.

For a moment, all thoughts of danger and duty vanished, replaced by a burning need to be close to one another.

His hands began roaming across her skintight bodysuit. One hand cupped her ass, pulling her hips closer to the edge of the table, while the other slid up to fondle her breast. She gasped into his mouth. The hard ridges of his bare torso fit perfectly against her own curves as he ground his hips against hers, the friction sending sparks of heat down her spine.

It was when she accidentally pressed her fingers against his injured back, causing him to flinch slightly, that common sense came flooding back to her.

She placed a hand on his chest and broke off the kiss, breathless and flushed.

"We… we shouldn't," she whispered with a mix of desire and conflict.

He was silent for a moment, his chest rising and falling heavily, his arms still holding her close. She saw the slightest hint of disappointment on his face.

"No intra-departmental relations, remember?" she said, hoping that the reminder would be enough to persuade him—and herself—to not go any further.

Contrary to her words, though, her own mind and body were betraying her by the second, egging her to give in to the possibility of a hot, no-strings-attached sex with a best-in-class operative… who happened to look and taste like a blond demigod.

He seemed to sense her inner struggles, and the battle played out across his own face. His breathing was still heavy, his hands lingering on her waist, his body so close she could feel his heat. For a moment, she thought he might ignore her words, push her over the edge she was teetering on.

Instead, with a resigned exhale, he stepped back. "You're right," he said, his hands reluctantly leaving her body. "Forgive me, I got carried away." He offered her a hand, helping her down from the table. "We wouldn't want to make things awkward between us."

She released a breath she hadn't realised she'd been holding. *More awkward, you mean,* was what she wanted to say. Instead, she took his hand and got up.

"Sorry, Luna," he repeated, his voice genuine.

"That's quite alright," she replied, her tone softer than she intended. She noted her own sense of disappointment, but pushed it aside. "Let's cool off and debrief." She added quickly, "Separate showers."

They both cracked up and laughed, the tenseness easing, their newfound camaraderie a welcome break from the intense encounter.

All in all, it was a good night's work, with the both of them silently hoping that would be enough to carry them through the turmoil that was to come.

6 / OKTO

Bishop wandered through the markets, the air alive with the scent of fresh spices and the voices of vendors calling out their wares.

She and Helix had divided their tasks for the day. He was deep in the throes of gathering intel on Lantau Island, while she was tasked with something less urgent.

She needed this; the space to breathe, to focus on the cold, hard facts of the mission and not the simmering connection that seemed to follow them everywhere. Being around Helix had always been complicated—now it was on the verge of being dangerous.

With a few hours of downtime on her hands, she had decided to familiarise herself with the neighbourhood around their high-rise, mapping out escape routes and potential hideouts in case things went south.

Her attention was drawn to an elderly woman who approached her with a warm, toothy smile. The woman held out a tray of delicate jewellery.

"Earrings, bracelets, miss?"

Bishop glanced at the array, politely shaking her head. "No, thank you." But her eyes lingered just a little too long on one of the pieces on display, which didn't go unnoticed.

"Oh, this one is perfect for you!!" The woman insisted, picking up the pair of glinting earrings. "Moonstone, symbol of fertility!"

The comment brought a small smile to Bishop's lips. How fitting, she thought, noting the subtle irony with her real name. Just then, her phone buzzed; it was an encrypted voice call.

She answered while excusing herself from the jewellery vendor. "Hello?"

There was a brief pause before Snatch's voice came through from the other end, his tone uncharacteristically grave. "*Hi, Luna.*"

"Rob? Isn't it early morning in London? How are you doing?"

"*Not great, unfortunately,*" he replied, the weight of his words seeping through the call.

Bishop's amusement faded. "Is everything alright?"

At the other end of the line, Snatch casually sat at his cubicle at the MI6 headquarters, coffee in hand. Morning light seeped through the windows and bathed one side of his face with blinding lights, so he turned his chair around and propped both feet up on his desk.

"I've been going through some Orion data," he said, "I found several communications and movements that are inconsistent with Helix's reported activities. There are some discrepancies, things that don't add up."

Bishop was puzzled. "What sort of discrepancies?"

Snatch took a deep breath. "Things like him going off-grid for very short periods, making contact with unknown entities."

Bishop's heart skipped a beat. *What?*

"He's very subtle, Luna—so subtle that Orion missed it," Snatch said again. "I only stumbled across this because I was researching something else entirely. Some hacked Soviet lines had mentions of our agents' codenames, some of which happened to be the ones who had been recently killed in Hong Kong.

"However, they also mentioned an asset by the name of 'Okto' a few times. It rang alarm bells for me because 'Okto' was…"

"Helix's old codename from German intelligence," muttered Bishop, recollecting the extensive amount of files she had studied before the mission. She felt a chill run down her spine.

Snatch's voice pulled her back. "At first, I thought it was just a coincidence, but when I cross-referenced it with his recent activities, it didn't look good. It all lines up too perfectly. Has he ever acted suspiciously while you've been there?"

Bishop thought far and wide. She recalled how Helix had been proactive to take the lead when investigating Cheyevskaya and the Zong Triad, but when it came to dealing with Sluzhba agents, he always seemed to hold back. It was *she* who took down Karamov, and it was *her* finger on the trigger, ready to fire at Vareleva. There had been moments when something about him just felt… off, as if he was deliberately avoiding direct confrontation with Soviet operatives.

"Yes, actually. Rob, have you informed Chief Adamson about this?"

"Not yet. The evidence I have so far is not conclusive—"

"—Let me find a proof for you then," she interjected.

Snatch gave a long exhale. "Okay, but you need to be extra careful. If he really is a double agent, you are in serious danger."

His fingers danced on the projected keyboard before tapping Enter. "I'm sending you all the data I've flagged. Cross-reference it with what you know and see if there's anything we've missed. We can't afford to jump to conclusions without a solid proof."

"Of course. Thanks, Snatch," she replied. As she hung up, determination surged within her.

I knew he was trouble, Bishop thought to herself, her market jaunt now forgotten. She had to tread carefully against a spook of his calibre. She needed a plan, and fast.

She looked back at the smiling old woman at her jewellery stall, cogs turning in her brain.

Helix slipped into the apartment quietly, the door clicking shut behind him. The digital clock on the wall blinked just after 1 a.m. His motorcycle helmet hung from one hand, and he shrugged off his leather jacket, the scent of the night air still clinging to it.

Clarke had refused to issue them another car after the last one was lost in the chase, so he had to make do with the station's standard-issue bike. It was the first time he'd ridden again in years, and the muscle memory came back with a rush of adrenaline and nostalgia. It was efficient, but exhausting having to swerve around Hong Kong traffic.

He placed the helmet and jacket on the small table near the entrance and made his way to the kitchen, thinking a strong cup of coffee would shake off the chill. The machine hummed to life as he turned it on, the familiar aroma beginning to fill the space.

He opened the fridge while waiting for the coffee to brew, and heard a soft rustle behind him. Bishop appeared in the doorway, her figure silhouetted by the light from the hall. She was wearing a short silk dressing gown that clung to her form, her hair falling loosely around her shoulders.

"You're late, Alex," she said, her voice a blend of reproach and invitation.

He took in the sight of her, a smile curling. "If I'd known you were waiting for me, I would've come home sooner." His tone was casual, but there was the faintest hint of a smoulder in his tired eyes. "May I have some of your vodka?" he asked, pointing at the bottle of Stolichnaya on the shelf.

"Help yourself," she replied, her eyes never leaving him, "I'll have one too."

He closed the fridge and pried open the seal. "Seems like just last week I saw a full bottle in the fridge. Already gone?"

"Yep," she replied, bending over to grab a couple of clean cups from the dishwasher. "What can I do? I need it to stay awake in this dark, dark world…"

He was about to tease her about having an alcohol problem, but the sight of her made him stop. The faint light played across her skin and he caught himself staring, his eyes tracing her neckline, her delicate moonstone earrings, and the swell of cleavage peeking out from under her camisole.

She poured coffee into the cups and he stepped closer. "Single or double?" he asked.

"Just a single," she answered, the slightest hint of a smile touching her lips, as he obliged and poured the spirit into her coffee.

At the dining table, Helix tapped his tablet, conjuring a hologram with a detailed map of the casino onto the table's polished surface. The soft blue glow illuminated the dining room and their faces.

"So how did it go, and what took you so long?" Bishop asked, taking a seat in a chair.

He offered a tired but contented smile. "I went for a ride after the recon."

She didn't answer. That whole afternoon, she had dived into the data curated by Snatch, sifting through Helix's communications, timestamps, and locations. The deeper she went, the more uneasy she became. Patterns began to emerge, pointing to a web of deceit that threatened to unravel everything she—*they*—had worked for. The implications were too severe to ignore.

"It wasn't bad though, I got decent intel," Helix said again, his gaze shifting from her to the floating map. "This is the newly opened 'Casinopolis' on Lantau Island."

He paused, tapping an area of the map with a finger. "As Sylvia said, the Zong Triad frequently hosts Russian mafia leaders and Chinese business tycoons there."

His fingers traced over different sections of the casino. "The complex draws inspiration from the ancient Acropolis, with three unique gambling areas open to the public. Orion had already mapped out most of the public spaces with unsettling accuracy, capturing every shadow. I went around the back to map out the rest."

He gestured at the different sections. "The Parthenon Hall is lined with rows of pachinko machines, and the Dionysus Hall has dedicated blackjack and roulette tables. But we're mostly interested in the Pericles Lounge, the exclusive poker area where entry alone costs at least 50,000 Hong Kong dollars."

His eyes locked onto hers. "Safin always opens a table there every Thursday night. So, let's split up and tackle this separately."

Bishop leaned against the table, arms crossed. "What does that mean? Am I not coming with you?"

Helix pointed to an isolated area of the casino, away from the main sections. "You're more valuable here. The VIP lounge needs a waitress who can blend in."

She pouted. "Why do you always get the better job?"

His eyes sparkled with amusement. "Your cover is always flawless. Besides, you'll look better in a *qipao* than I would." He pulled up a photo of a casino waitress in a Chinese dress that he'd snapped earlier. As he imagined her in that same dress, his thoughts wandered to how thc fabric would accentuate her figure, the high slit teasing with every step she took...

"Seriously? That's your excuse?" she shot back, snapping him back to reality. With a heavy sigh, she muttered, "If I'd known, I wouldn't have gone through hell to secure that 80,000 dollars."

Helix raised an eyebrow. "Eighty-thousand?"

"Yeah," she replied, feigning nonchalance. "Clarke gave us 80,000 dollars to use in the Pericles Lounge, but told me not to blow it all at once."

This time, Helix's surprise was genuine. "Hang on, Clarke, the penny-pincher, gave you an extra 30,000?"

"Mm-hmm," Bishop teased, a smirk playing on her lips. "Never underestimate the negotiation skills of a determined Chinese."

He retorted: "Aren't you only half-Cantonese? Even my Mandarin's better than yours."

She pouted again, a gesture he found increasingly endearing. He was right; her vibe and demeanour were distinctly English, except for those almond eyes and light olive complexion—features that kept him captivated. He took a slow sip of his spiked coffee.

Bishop let out a long, thoughtful sigh and shrugged. "You think Clarke fancies me?"

The coffee seemed to go down the wrong way, making him cough before bursting into laughter. "If that's the case, Luna, my condolences."

Her voice dropped to a teasing whisper, her lips almost brushing his ear. "What's the matter, Alex? Afraid of a little competition?"

He chuckled, his warm breath grazing her skin. "There's no competition. Clarke's old enough to be your father."

She raised an eyebrow. "I could say the same about you and Chief Adamson."

His smile faded. "You're still going on about me and the Chief?"

"Oh, come on," she teased, her tone light but her eyes unsmiling. "She talks about you like you're the best thing there is. I'm just curious." Their faces were just inches apart now.

He pondered the sudden shift in her behaviour. Just the other night, she had been steadfast in maintaining a professional distance that had left him puzzled and somewhat frustrated. Now, she was encouraging him with soft whispers, playing coyly with her hair and tilting her bare neck—clear signs of seduction. Had something changed, or was there another motive behind her newfound flirtation?

He quickly decided that if she was opening this door, he might as well take his shot.

"Could it be… that my moon goddess is actually jealous?"

Her breath caught at the affectionate nickname and the sensation of his fingers on her face. She'd always resisted his pull, no matter how tempting it had been, no matter how damn handsome he was. But now, if seducing him could help her uncover his secrets, wasn't it her duty to try?

Unfortunately, she couldn't help reverting back to her original programming. Just as their lips were about to touch, she quipped, "I'm just curious why Chief Adamson trusts you so much… when it's clear your other superiors don't."

His irritation flared. Her sudden openness had caught him off guard, but it seemed she was only playing a game.

Before she could say another word, he grabbed her arm and closed the distance between them, his lips crashing against hers. The bitterness of coffee mixed with vodka and a faint trace of tobacco filled her mouth, and she surprisingly found it quite pleasant. The heat of his body against hers melted her into a passionate reciprocation as their kiss deepened.

But he abruptly pulled away, his eyes icy.

"If you're that curious, Luna, why don't you ask her yourself?"

She was at a loss for words as he collected his tablet, spun around, and strode purposefully towards the door, his back stiff. The room felt heavy and her thoughts were in a whirl.

As the sound of his footsteps receded down the hallway, she finally managed to shake off the distraction that was his taste. She fumed, his dismissive words still echoing.

Damn you, Helix, she thought bitterly. *I will expose your secret… if it's the last thing I do.*

// Lantau Island //

Inside Casinopolis, the crystal chandeliers reflected light off the polished marble floors while a constant humdrum of activity filled the air—roulette wheels spun, cards shuffled, and dice clattered against the felt tables.

The chatter of gamblers, mixed with the occasional cheer or groan of defeat, created an atmosphere of relentless energy. High-rollers occupied the elite gambling lounges, while the less fortunate tried their luck in the Parthenon Hall.

At the back of the house, Bishop blended with the shadows. She wore the sleek, black Chinese dress uniform that she'd procured from a staff locker, her dark hair pinned up, and she looked every bit the part of a waitress—even if the dress was a size too small.

She took advantage of an unfolding scene—some short-fused down-on-their-luck patrons causing a ruckus—that had sent security guards rushing out to manage the commotion. She slipped into the security office to retrieve a set of access cards.

While inside, she scanned the security monitors, her eyes darting over the feeds. There were too many cameras, too many rooms. She should be focusing solely on the VIP lounge, but she also needed to know where Helix was and what he was up to… because she had no idea if she could trust him.

In contrast to the other gambling halls, the Pericles Lounge was quieter and more refined—a place where deals were made over high-stakes poker games.

At one of the tables, a group of Chinese businessmen was engaged in a game, their business talk at times interrupted by bluffs and calculation of odds. Among them was Safin, the only Russian there, an older man who commanded respect despite his soft-spoken voice.

"I hear thrifty Lu's business is on the rise again, eh?" one of the businessmen, Zhou, commented with a sly smile.

"I've heard the same," another added, "but isn't that because of your intervention, Mister Safin? You're too kind to him."

"Not at all, Zhou," Safin replied calmly. "There's a Russian saying, 'Even God likes trinity'. It means, if you try three times, even someone as unlucky as Lu can succeed."

"Classic Safin!" Zhou laughed, shaking his head.

But Safin added: "Too bad the same can't be said for his daughter, with a new husband every year …"

The table broke into laughter. "Your sharp tongue hasn't changed, Safin!" Zhou retorted with a grin.

As they continued the game, Helix walked past, wearing a black tuxedo but with hair clipped in a tight man bun to go with his cover as a Gen-Z trust fund baby.

"*Gospodin* Safin?" Helix said, stopping in his tracks. "What a coincidence to run into you here!"

Safin recognised him instantly, and got up from his seat. "Oh! If I'm not mistaken, Mister William Truss, from Pennsylvania?"

Helix gave a modest smile. "I didn't expect you to remember me, *gospodin*!"

"Of course I remember!" Safin turned to Zhou, who was watching curiously. "Hey Zhou, do you remember the young man I told you about? The one who nearly bankrupted me playing mahjong in Shanghai last year? This is him!"

Helix chuckled, downplaying the memory. "Please, *gospodin*. I was just lucky that day."

Zhou eyed Helix with mock seriousness. "Uh-oh, Safin! Since when has your Lady Luck started favouring the young?"

Safin, with a smirk, turned to Helix again. "By the way, William, have you found a table yet?"

"Not yet, but it's no big deal—"

"Nonsense!" Safin cut him off. "Join us! Let's see if you can repay me for that loss…"

Helix obliged. He scanned the table, his mind running a quick tally of the men seated around it.

Grigory Safin, of course, was the Soviet conglomerate with significant ties to the Cheyevskaya Group in Hong Kong. Bernard Zhou, his close ally, was a prominent venture capitalist and the largest donor to the Chinese Nationalist League. Then there were the old moneyed elites from oil, manufacturing, and the eco sectors. With backers like these behind Jiang Yaozu, it was no surprise the election seemed like a foregone conclusion.

The scent of luxury and power hung heavy in the VIP area. Bishop pushed the cart carefully, the expensive bottles of champagne and other high-end liquors clinking softly against each other.

As she approached the guarded entrance, a group of Triad members stood like statues, their presence intimidating.

"Excuse me," Bishop said, her voice smooth and professional. "On behalf of the casino management, we have a special treat for our VIP guests."

One of the guards, his eyes narrowing at the sight of the liquor, ogled her, his gaze settling on the high-slit uniform she wore.

A smirk tugged at the corner of his mouth as he replied, "What a treat. Too bad, there's an important meeting inside that can't be interrupted. So, just leave your special treat here with us, okay?"

Bishop hesitated for a moment, then nodded, "Sure."

As she prepared her next move, a man stepped out of the shadows. His darkened glasses reflected the ambient light, and his long coat swayed slightly as he moved. His features were strikingly handsome, distinctly East Asian, and he exuded an air of authority.

"What's going on?" he asked, his voice calm yet commanding.

The guard quickly straightened up and answered, "Oh, boss! This waitress said..."

Bishop's ears immediately perked up as the men conversed. *Why are they speaking Mandarin? Are they not the Zong Triad?*

The mysterious man's gaze shifted to the champagne bottles on the cart. "From the management, huh? Might as well, Miss Xiao has been waiting long enough."

He turned to his men, his tone laced with reprimand. "Why are you just standing there? Search the waitress, then bring the drinks inside!"

The guards jumped to action. "Y-yes, boss!" they stammered.

Bishop remained composed as they quickly and efficiently searched her. Finding nothing suspicious, they allowed her to proceed. The tall man escorted her into the VIP room.

"Miss Xiao..." the man said as they entered.

From the shadows, a woman's voice responded, laced with impatience. "Safin hasn't shown up—Wan?"

"Not yet," the man replied. "But there's a little treat from management."

As Bishop moved closer, she caught a glimpse of the woman speaking, recognition dawning on her. She had seen her face before, in one of her case files. Xiao Mingzu, also known as the 'Dragon Lady', was a high-ranking figure in Taiwan's underworld.

The Dragon Lady stared at the champagne with a mixture of indifference and disappointment. "How disappointing," she murmured. "Is time as cheap as life for these Russians?"

A soft laugh broke the tenseness. Another man, Chinese, dressed in a tailored suit, reassured her. "Don't worry, Miss Xiao. For as long as he has been dealing with us in the 'Third Bureau', Mister Safin never disappoints..."

As Bishop poured the drinks, her thoughts were in a whirl. Third Bureau in this case could only mean one thing: the department within Chinese intelligence that focused on Taiwan.

She kept her hands steady. The Zong Triad, the Cheyevskaya, the Taiwanese triad, and now anti-Taiwanese Chinese intelligence—these groups weren't supposed to be allies. She kept her eyes and ears open, hoping that every word and action in this room could help solve the puzzle she couldn't yet see the full picture of.

Back in Pericles Lounge, Safin and his cronies, with the addition of Helix, were deeply engrossed in their game. The clinking of chips, the shuffle of cards, and the low murmur of conversation created a cocoon of intensity. But the mood was soon interrupted when an assistant approached Safin, his demeanour apologetic.

"I'm very sorry, *gospodin*," the assistant began, his voice low and respectful, "but your guest has been waiting for quite some time."

Safin's expression darkened with disappointment. "What a shame, the game was just getting interesting..." He sighed, then addressed the table, "Gentlemen, I'm afraid I have to leave you here tonight."

One of the men protested, "You can't leave yet, Mister Safin!"

Safin offered a regretful smile as he replied, "I apologise, Mister Wu. My assistant Mikhail will handle all the accounts."

But before Mikhail could step in, a new voice cut through the room, "That won't be necessary, *dyadya*... I'll take your place."

Safin's assistant tensed and leaned in to warn, "Don't, *gospodin*!"

However, Safin waved off the concern. "If that's what you want, Pyotr," he said with a resigned nod.

Turning to the others around the table, he introduced the newcomer. "Gentlemen, I'm sure you're all acquainted with my nephew, Pyotr?"

Helix sized up the young man taking Safin's place. *Pyotr Dorodny...* he was another protégé within the Cheyevskaya syndicate in Hong Kong. Unlike Sylvia's gentle husband Nicolai, who heavily relied on his wife's iron will, Dorodny operated with ruthlessness, often disregarding the organisation's norms. Ironically, he might be the one most capable of pulling Cheyevskaya out of the nationalist hell China was currently in.

Dorodny settled into Safin's seat, his movements deliberate, caressing the arm of the chair as if it were a throne. "Go on, *dyadya*," he said dismissively. "You wouldn't want to keep the Dragon Lady waiting, would you?"

Helix noted how even Safin had to pander to him. Dorodny then turned his attention to the game. "Now, where were we? Oh, yes. I'll bet $20,000 on the fourth card."

The reactions around the table were immediate, and not pleased.

"He hasn't even seen the cards…" one of the men muttered under his breath.

"He's playing with Safin's money, isn't he?" another chimed in, disdain clear in his voice.

Dorodny, unbothered, taunted them, "Come on now, no need to hold back—"

Before he could finish, Helix, seated next to him, called, "I call, $30,000."

Others at the table quickly followed suit. "Call!" "I'm in too!"

Dorodny's eyes locked onto Helix, a smirk playing on his lips. He leaned in closer, his voice dropping to a conspiratorial whisper. "You've got quite the money to spend, friend. No surprise, given that you serve two masters, isn't that right—Okto?"

Helix's expression changed at the mention of the name, but he quickly regained composure. "You seem well-versed in Moscow's little games, *gospodin.* Doesn't Levski specifically tell his men not to collaborate with government spies?"

The dealer revealed the fourth card, the Queen of Spades.

Dorodny, his tone still casual, added, "Well, Levski doesn't need to know, does he? Relax, I'm not here to rattle you. Quite the opposite, actually—your handler asked me to pass this along."

He discreetly handed Helix a piece of holographic card as the dealer announced the bets for the fifth and final card.

“$45,000!” someone called.

“I call $50,000!” another followed.

Helix took the card, its transparent surface hiding a slew of encrypted messages, as the game continued around him.

7 / THE HUNT

Bishop stepped into the MRT station on Lantau Island, the cool air brushing against her skin as she moved through the bustling crowds. The station, with its bright lights and ceaseless activity, was a stark contrast to the growing concern within her.

The deadline has passed, she thought, glancing around, her eyes scanning the sea of faces. *But there's still no sign of Helix. I might as well head back. There's so much I need to report...*

Unbeknownst to her, a pair of eyes locked onto her every move, tracking her with deliberateness.

"The target has appeared," a voice murmured into a hidden communication device.

"Good," came the reply, cold and commanding. It was Vareleva, her tone laced with anticipation. "Leave the rest to us."

On the other side of the island, Helix stood on the grand forum outside Casinopolis, its façade bearing a striking resemblance to the Parthenon but decorated with gaudy statues with gold trimmings. From the mainland, the city lights flickered like distant stars.

As he placed an earpiece in his ear, the voice on the other end greeted him in Russian, tense and irritated.

"Didn't I tell you never to contact me like this, Okto?"

Helix's voice was calm as he responded, also in Russian: "I've just received a message from the station in Hong Kong. They're ordering me to step back from all missions for the time being."

The man on the line responded without a trace of emotion, "Sounds like good advice."

Helix's brow furrowed. "What does Kuznetsov mean by 'stay away from the hunt', Stoki?"

The man's tone turned grave as he explained, "The Fifth Column has lost assets again—this time, two American agents. Unfortunately, a few of Kuznetsov's men have also fallen victim."

Helix could feel the weight of the situation growing as his handler added with emphasis, "He's now deploying his best forces to hunt down the perpetrators—your partner included."

Helix sighed, feeling a pang of regret. "I see. That's a shame... the girl could have been a highly effective asset."

Stoki's voice was sharp as he warned, "Watch your words, Okto. Kuznetsov is already at the edge of his patience. Don't provoke him further, or I won't be able to guarantee your safety there."

Helix quickly acknowledged his mistake. "I understand." He ended the call, slipping his phone back into his pocket.

He had thought it was strange that Dorodny had so carelessly exposed himself as a Sluzhba intermediary; the fallout would be catastrophic if Levski ever found out.

But he didn't dwell on it too long, his thoughts drifting instead to his partner.

I hope you make it through, Bishop, he thought, the words echoing in his mind with a weight that surprised him.

`Welcome to Tung Chung. Please do not leave your belongings on the train.`

The announcement sliced through the ambient noise of the busy platform. Bishop got on the train and stood still, her gaze sweeping over the throngs of commuters. Tugging her hoodie lower over her head, she allowed the fabric to cast a shadow across her face, blending into the crowd with effortlessness. Her senses were on high alert, each one attuned to the subtle signals of danger.

Something's wrong, she thought. *I've felt eyes on me ever since I left the casino.*

`The next station is Lai King. Please keep an eye on your belongings at all times.`

The PA system blared again as she reached the interchange station. Bishop weaved through the crowd with an air of nonchalance. Her mind, however, was busy speculating. *Could they be Soviet agents?*

`Train approaching platform 4.`

Bishop's eyes narrowed, calculating her next move as a train pulled into the station. The doors slid open with a hiss, and without hesitation, she slipped inside, vanishing into the mass of passengers just as the train began its journey.

One of the female operatives on the platform cursed under her breath as she caught a fleeting glimpse of Bishop boarding the train. "Vareleva, I see the target! She's on the Tsuen Wan Line, heading south!" Her voice crackled as she spoke into her earpiece.

Vareleva's response was sharp, decisive. "Isn't Dimi nearby?"

A third voice, Dimi's, cut in, calm and confident. "I've got her," he confirmed, eyes locked onto Bishop as he followed her onto the same train carriage. He kept a safe distance, watching her every move as the train rattled along the tracks.

When the train came to a stop at Yau Ma Tei, Bishop stepped off, her pace unhurried as she moved toward the exit. Dimi trailed her, his hand hovering near his concealed weapon, ready for any sign of trouble. She led him through the crowded station, her movements deliberate as she manoeuvred toward a less populated exit. The narrow dark alley she entered offered the perfect cover.

Dimi hesitated as he stepped into the alley, his gun now drawn. The oppressive silence pressed in around him.

Without warning, a shadow above him shifted. Bishop, perched silently on an emergency staircase, leaped down, landing with cat-like agility behind him. Before Dimi could react, she wrapped an arm around his neck, snapping it with a swift, brutal motion. His body crumpled to the ground, the gun slipping from his lifeless hand.

The frantic voices coming from Dimi's earpiece caught her attention. "Dimi, what's happening? Dmitri?!"

The urgency in their tone left no doubt—they were closing in. Bishop picked up Dimi's gun and steeled herself for what was to come. The silence of the alley was shattered as her other attackers stormed in, guns drawn.

Bishop ducked behind a dumpster as bullets ricocheted off the walls, sharp, metallic pings filling the confined space. She returned fire with lethal accuracy, each shot finding its mark. They pressed forward, relentless in their pursuit. One by one, they fell, but they kept coming, determined to take her down. Her breath came in controlled bursts while she reloaded, her mind working through the maze of possible escape routes.

As the last agent hit the ground, Bishop heard the ominous sound of more footsteps approaching. Her eyes flicked to the narrow passage leading to the street beyond, but it was too risky. She pressed herself against the wall as she prepared for another wave of attacks.

After leaving Casinopolis, Helix sauntered through the park, the sparse streetlights casting long shadows on the pavement. The electronic cigarette between his lips glowed faintly, its ember the only sign of life in the otherwise deserted park.

Zhao had been tailing him since that phone call. He had known it from the start, but had let the man follow, drawing him into the darkness where the balance of power could shift.

Helix waited, biding his time. Then, with a sudden burst of movement, he spun on his heel, racing back towards Zhao. As he closed the distance, he flung his coat forward, the heavy fabric billowing in the air to obscure his true intentions. In a flash, his dagger was out, slicing through the coat with indifference. Zhao barely had time to react before the cold steel was pressed against his throat.

"You're one of Vareleva's men, aren't you?" Helix's voice was low, dangerous. "Wasn't it enough to chase us around Hong Kong in your car?"

Zhao's eyes widened as the dagger bit into his skin. But he tried to keep his composure. "Don't play dumb, Okto. You know exactly how much trouble you and your 'fifth columnist' friends have caused. Backed by Moscow, no one can touch or question your operations, no matter the circumstances."

He swallowed hard when he felt the blade pressing against his windpipe. "So many of us have died protecting your secrets. But what have we gained? Kuznetsov won't tolerate it any longer. Starting today, the Soviet station in Hong Kong is no longer your ally—"

Zhao's words were abruptly cut off by the sharp crack of a gunshot. Blood sprayed as a bullet tore through his skull, and he crumpled to the ground.

Helix didn't hesitate. He lunged into the bushes, taking cover as more bullets rained down on the spot where he had been standing just moments before. He assessed the situation, adrenaline sharpening his instincts.

How many of them are there? Have they surrounded the area? More importantly, who sent them?

He listened closely, the gunfire growing louder as his attackers moved in. He knew only one thing for certain. As he was still alive, that would mean these men weren't trained killers.

Reaching into his pocket, he pulled out his fibre-optic glasses and slid them on, activating night vision. The world around him shifted into shades of green. He shot out the nearest streetlights with silenced rounds, plunging the area into darkness.

He moved swiftly, his footsteps silent on the grass as he closed in on the first of his attackers. The man hadn't even realised danger was there before the knife found his throat, silencing him forever.

The next target was behind a tree, firing blindly into the darkness. Helix approached from behind, wrapping an arm around the man's neck and snapping it with a quick, practised movement.

He continued his deadly dance through the park, systematically eliminating his hunters. He moved with the coolness of a predator, each kill quick and efficient. A knife to the ribs here, a bullet to the head there—no wasted movements, no hesitation.

The last of the attackers attempted to flee, realising too late that they were outmatched. Helix's cold, calculated gaze tracked him through the darkness. He hurled his tanto blade; the dagger slicing through the air and finding its mark. The man collapsed, his body hitting the ground with a dull thud.

Helix stood over the fallen bodies, his breathing steady, his heart rate barely elevated. He removed the glasses, the night vision fading as the world returned to its natural shadows, then went over to retrieve his knife. For a moment, he simply stood there, listening to the eerie silence that had settled over the park.

They didn't come for me, he thought, *but they didn't expect to face me either.*

Making his way through the aftermath of the skirmish, he noticed the distinctive tattoos inked onto the wrists of his fallen attackers. The symbol was unmistakable—a dragon entwined with a stylized 'Z'. The mark of the Zong Triad. He paused. The triad's reach was broader than he had anticipated, their involvement a chilling reminder of the intricate web of alliances surrounding him.

"This way!" The urgent shout reverberated through the narrow alley, the heavy thuds of boots closing in. Vareleva, flanked by several of her underlings, spotted one of their own slumped near a dumpster. "Xin!" one of them called out, panic lacing his voice. "Are you alright?"

A groan escaped the man's lips, his consciousness flickering in and out. He was still alive, but just barely.

Vareleva's eyes hardened as she barked, "Get him to the observation point immediately." Her gaze dropped to the ground, where a faint trail of blood glistened under the dim streetlight. Her jaw tightened as she snapped out orders, "Irina, Yang, move ahead and follow that trail."

She brought a hand to her earpiece. "Zhao, what's your status?" she demanded, her voice sharp and commanding.

Silence.

"Zhao?" she repeated, irritation edging into her tone.

A moment later, a voice crackled through the earpiece—not Zhao's, but Helix's. "*Your friend is dead.*"

Vareleva's fury ignited, a blaze of anger flashing in her eyes. "You!"

Helix sat motionless on a bench near the fountain outside Tung Chung Metro Station. He had a cigarette in hand, and the crowd moved around him in a blur. "I didn't kill him," he replied. "It was the Zong Triad. I believe they're trying to send a warning to anyone who might oppose Jiang's control. Looks like you're not the only ones out hunting tonight..."

There was a brief pause before he began again, his voice taking on a graver note.

"Vareleva, pull back your people. If the triad or Jiang gets concrete proof that your side is colluding with Liu, the consequences will be severe."

Vareleva's knuckles turned white with rage. "Enough, Helix—Okto, or whatever name you're going by these days. Instead of meddling in our affairs, why don't you go back and kiss up to your Moscow overlords?"

Her voice dripped with venom, every word calculated to cut deep. "Last I heard, most of your comrades have already died honourable deaths. My advice? Start praying. Because the moment Moscow decides you're no longer useful, I'll be the one to end you."

With a sharp flick of her wrist, she ended the call, seething.

Helix removed his earpiece and gazed up at the sky. The full moon hung high above, casting a silvery light over the fountain.

Luna. Her name crossed his mind, unbidden. She was out there, alone.

His expression hardened, resolve setting in like steel. His decision was becoming clearer by the second. He wouldn't be cowed by threats, not from anyone in Moscow, and certainly not from local Sluzhba agents.

He needed to find Bishop, consequences be damned.

With a final glance at the moon, he turned on his heel.

As Bishop rounded another corner, her earpiece switched on. "*Bishop, are you there?*" Helix's voice sliced through, jarring her from the survival mode she'd been running on for the past hour. Her thoughts had blurred into a single, desperate focus on staying alive, but now they scattered as exhaustion crept in.

She pulled out her phone, her breath catching as she saw his location displayed on the screen. He was still on Lantau Island.

Confusion battled with suspicion in her mind, a fear settling in as she realised he could also see where she was. *Could he be the one giving away my position?* The possibility chilled her, the thought that her own device—and partner—might be the source of her problems.

Before she could fully process the implications, his voice broke through again. "*Luna, if you're okay, answer me!*"

She hesitated, mistrust growing like a dark cloud. Then, following a split-second decision, she hurled the phone into the darkness of the alley. It clattered to the ground, disappearing into the shadows as she pressed forward, determined to find a way out without the risk of further betrayal.

But the night wasn't done with her yet. Some time later, as she descended down a narrow, winding path, a sharp pain exploded in her upper left arm. She barely registered the gunshot before the impact sent her sprawling to the ground, her face slamming into the cold, wet pavement. The bullet had hit a metal railing and ricocheted straight into her. She lay there, stunned and breathless.

A heavy boot pressed down on her back, and she felt the cold steel of an operative's gun barrel against her neck.

"Don't even think about it," a rough male voice warned.

Vareleva emerged from the shadows, standing on a ledge above them, her gun trained on Bishop as well. Her voice dripped with cold menace. "You think you can escape after spilling so much of our blood? Foolish woman."

Quick as lightning and ignoring the searing pain in her arm, Bishop twisted around, a small knife slipping into her hand. With a sharp upward slash, she caught the man holding her off guard, the blade slicing across his face. He screamed in pain, staggering back as blood poured from the wound. Bishop didn't hesitate—she leaped forward, adrenaline overriding the agony.

Yet before she could gain any ground, a shot rang out. A bullet slammed into her thigh, dropping her to the ground once again. In an instant, Vareleva was on top of her, pinning her down with the full weight of her body.

"Bitch!" Vareleva spat, pressing the cold barrel of her gun against Bishop's temple. "Should I torture you first, or just put you out of your misery?"

Bishop, writhing in pain, glared up at her, defiance burning in her eyes. "Just go ahead and kill me! Kill me like you did those British agents!"

Vareleva's expression twisted as she let out a mocking laughter. "Is that the lie they fed you? On the contrary, darling, do you know how many valuable assets we had to sacrifice to protect those damned double agents?"

Confusion flickered in Bishop's eyes, but she forced herself to ask, "Is one of them named 'Okto'?"

Vareleva's fury erupted. "No! Unfortunately, that idiot is still alive. And now I know why! It's because of weak agents like you who can't do anything even when the enemy is right beside you—"

A gunshot cracked through the air, cutting her off mid-sentence. Vareleva's body jerked violently as the bullet tore through the back of her head, killing her instantly.

The other operative—the one with the bloodied face—shouted her name, but another shot silenced him for good.

Bishop looked up, her vision blurring from the shock and fatigue, but she recognised the silhouette stepping out of the shadows, gun in hand. His presence was almost surreal, like a ghost materialising from the darkness. He walked over, holding something up in his hand—it was her broken phone, the one she had discarded far behind.

"Hey, Bishop..." Helix said, coldly, "This yours?"

The warmth of the blood seeping into her clothes, combined with the crushing weight of the dead woman on top of her, made it difficult to breathe. He must have heard everything. Her mind raced, trying to process the situation, but all she could feel was a deep sense of resignation. She was at his mercy now.

Unexpectedly, he lowered his gun. He crouched beside her, his expression unreadable. "Here I am, playing your babysitter once again."

With surprising gentleness, he pulled her away from Vareleva's body, propping her up and helping her to her feet despite her weakened state and her dead left thigh. "Come on, let's get you patched up."

She leaned on him for support, her thoughts spinning wildly. *Why is he helping me?* she wondered, glancing at the fresh scratches and wounds on his arms and face. *And where did those come from?*

As he led her away from the bloody scene, Snatch's words echoed ominously in her mind.

"Has he ever acted suspiciously while you were there, Luna?"

She stared at Helix, her thoughts a tangled mess. Everything about this man screamed suspicion. Yet, as she caught a glimpse of the two lifeless bodies behind her, blood pooling around them, the chilling realisation struck her—she should have been the one lying dead over there.

A haunting question filled her thoughts, one that she couldn't shake no matter how hard she tried. Would she be able to point her gun at him, when the time finally came?

8 / GRAVITY

In the lively staff kitchen of SIS headquarters at Vauxhall Cross, a group of analysts huddled around the counter, laughing as Jamie, the office comedian, delivered his latest joke.

"So, the Russian walks in, face covered in blood, and says: 'Do you see that electric pole over there?'"

The group leaned in, grinning. "Yeah, yeah, we see it!" they chimed in unison.

"Well, I didn't!" Jamie exclaimed with a dramatic shrug, sending the group into a chorus of laughter and groans.

Snatch, who had been casually sipping his tea nearby, chuckled and shook his head. "Jamie, you're just pole-ing our legs now," he quipped, earning a few more laughs as he set down his cup.

"I'm heading out now," Snatch added, glancing at his watch.

"Take care, Rob!" Jamie said, still grinning as Snatch waved and headed out the door.

"It's already four," Snatch muttered to himself, his brow furrowing slightly. "Has the Pyongyang material come in yet?"

Turning his attention towards the Central Planning office, Snatch spotted Chief Adamson, a rare sight in this part of the building.

Isn't that Luna's superior? he wondered. *What's a Chief of Special Operations doing here?*

With a sigh, he headed back to his desk, determined to concentrate on the task at hand. "Alright, work work work!" he said with renewed energy.

Suddenly, a hand on his shoulder made him turn around. He found himself face-to-face with the Director of the Secret Intelligence Service.

As usual, Michael Lester had an air of aggressive authority that instantly quieted the room. His skin was a deep, rich black, contrasting sharply with the shock of white hair that framed his features, the only outward sign of his advancing years.

"Busy as usual, Mister Church?" Lester's voice was smooth, yet carried an undertone of menace. "May I have a word with you?"

Bishop sat in the apartment's den, which doubled as a study, the faint city light filtering through the curtains and casting soft shadows on her bandaged arm and thigh. Her expression was tight as she spoke with Snatch on the screen in front of her.

"I'm sorry, what? Lester wants you to spy on Chief Adamson?"

Snatch's face reflected a mix of conflict and resignation. "Yeah, I was just as shocked. Apparently, Lester suspects Adamson might be leaking intel to the enemy. And he's heard about the discrepancy in Helix's data... He's suspicious because your Chief has been so supportive of her golden boy. It's making him think there's more going on."

"I can't believe it, Snatch," Bishop said, shaking her head. "The Chief of Special Operations wouldn't risk her position just to be a low-level informant. Besides, I think Lester is just threatened by Adamson's influence. After all, she's the only one who could rival him for the MI6 director position, right?"

Snatch lowered his tone. "Well, if you're looking for motives for betrayal..."

Bishop leaned in, curiosity piqued. "What are you talking about?"

Snatch sent an article to her screen. "This was the bombing of the British consulate in Beirut 33 years ago, when Adamson lost her diplomat husband and their young son. What wasn't publicly known was that her husband was under scrutiny by MI6 for espionage accusations. Adamson herself only joined the Service three years after that incident."

Bishop's face hardened. "Are you insinuating that my Chief has been a mole in MI6 all these years, with Helix as her accomplice?"

Snatch's tone grew defensive. "Don't get all worked up, it's just a theory. But anything is possible."

As Bishop studied Snatch's expression on the screen, her mind drifted back to the events of the other night. Against all odds, Helix had saved her from Vareleva and her minions. But the memory felt tainted with doubt.

"If that's the case," Bishop said, her voice strained, "what theory do you have about Helix saving my life? I'm afraid to think he only helped to win my trust."

Snatch leaned closer to the screen, his face filling the frame. "And? Did his tactics work?"

Bishop's face tightened, unresolved emotions swirling beneath her calm exterior.

Snatch's voice was firm. "Listen, Luna, you don't owe him anything. Don't let his cheap tricks make you feel like you do. In critical situations, you need to prioritise your own safety. Got it?"

Bishop nodded, but her mind was elsewhere. *It was more than just a cheap trick,* she thought, replaying the image of Helix killing Vareleva. *A desk agent can't grasp the risk Helix took to save me.*

Snatch's voice pulled her back to the present. "Don't dwell on it too much. Anything else I can help with?"

"Oh, right, I almost forgot!" Bishop quipped. She sent him a picture of a man—the charismatic gang leader she'd encountered at Casinopolis. "Could you check the profile on this agent? His name is Julian Soh. He's an undercover CIA operative who'll be assisting us at the British consulate charity auction on Friday."

Snatch's reaction was immediate and intense. "You're still working in that state?!" he protested, pointing at her bandaged arm and thigh.

Bishop's response was steady. "The Hong Kong station is short-staffed. Besides, Clarke only tasked us with perimeter surveillance."

"Still!" His frustration was evident. "You should be resting and healing!"

She tried to reassure him. "It's fine. Just help me with the profile, okay? I'm curious about Agent Soh. I spoke with him during the briefing earlier today. We met during my last stakeout. He managed to infiltrate the Xiao Group and became a trusted aide to the Dragon Lady."

"Oh?" Snatch seemed intrigued. He studied the headshot and smirked. "He looks like your last ex, Luna. Tall, handsome, Asian—totally your type."

Bishop shot him a look, rolling her eyes. Her last boyfriend, a semi-professional athlete, had no idea what she really did for a living. She'd told him she was a physical therapist, which sort of explained her toned physique, but the scars were harder to justify. The relationship had been doomed from the start; the lies were just too much to keep up.

"I don't have a type, Rob. Even if I did, it would be 'not a spy'." *Or a double agent,* she mused silently.

He chuckled, scanning the intel. "The CIA seems fixated on Taiwan for this election. They have undercover agents all over the place."

"Not just the CIA," Bishop said, shaking her head. "The Sluzhba and MI6 are also interested. Clarke even postponed the investigation into his murdered agents and is now demanding a full report about Taiwan and Jiang."

Snatch laughed. "I don't envy you. Right then, get back to your report. I'll contact you if there are any updates. And please go on sick leave if your wounds aren't healing!"

"I'm fine for now. Thanks, Snatch," Bishop said, gratitude in her voice.

"Anytime. Don't forget our dinner plans!"

"Absolutely. See you soon," she said, ending the call.

Bishop leaned back against the chair, her fingers playing absent-mindedly with a stylus.

She stared at her blank holoscreen, her mind swirling with the fragments of her recent investigations. After a few days of downtime to nurse the hole in her thigh, the report she now needed to complete felt like an insurmountable task. With a deep breath, she began to dictate, the words coming slowly as she worked to organise her muddled thoughts.

"From the available clues, it is clear that Jiang and his party have formed an alliance with the Zong Triad and the Cheyevskaya Group in Hong Kong," she said, her eyes scanning the words as they appeared. "What complicates matters is the involvement of the Taiwanese mafia led by Xiao Mingzu, also known as the 'Dragon Lady'."

She dictated a few more findings, then ordered Orion to summarise.

`While the Dragon Lady seems to be showing increasing interest in Jiang's alliance, the motives and benefits for both parties through this alliance remain unclear.`

She stared at the text and irritation washed over her. This was hardly news.

She leaned back in her chair again as her eyes wandered around the room. The memory of the night Helix saved her came crashing back into her mind.

"Orion, restart dictation," she commanded. "After the Casinopolis recon, when Vareleva held me at gunpoint, she insisted that the Soviets weren't responsible for the deaths of our agents. But if that's true, then who was?"

She paused, remembering Vareleva's reaction when she mentioned the name 'Okto'. The intensity of that moment lived in her mind, but she decided to hold off on sharing this detail with Orion.

Until she could be certain that Okto was really Helix, and that he might be involved in the killings, she would rather keep her suspicion offline. There was also the possibility that Chief Adamson knew something, and a full-blown investigation could implicate her as well.

She reached for a pen and paper, sketching out maps and connections by hand. For now, the manual method would have to do.

A faint yellow light leaked from a tiny gap under the door, piercing the darkness of the den. Bishop was asleep at the desk, her head resting on one hand.

A thin nylon string snaked its way around her neck, brushing lightly against her skin. The sensation jerked her awake. As her eyes fluttered open, the nylon tightened around her throat, cutting off her breath. She gasped, her hands instinctively reaching up to fend off the constricting string, but the pain was immediate and sharp.

Struggling to breathe, she summoned all her willpower to twist and confront her attacker.

"Hello, darling," came Helix's voice, smooth and sinister. The garrotte was clutched tightly in his gloved hands, the ends pulled taut around her throat. She tried to speak, but only strangled gasps emerged.

Helix's smile widened. In one sweeping motion, he swung her body across the room, throwing her against the wooden cabinets. The impact hit her head hard and, before she could recover, he made his way to her.

She could see his eyes gleaming with malevolent delight in the dark. With his gun in hand, he traced its cold metal along the curve of her exposed midriff. The chill of the steel against her skin made her shudder.

The gun ascended to her neck, and Helix's thumb cocked the weapon with a crisp click. He lifted it, angling the barrel to her forehead. An evil smirk stretched across his face.

"It's been nice knowing you."

His finger pressed on the hammer. The room erupted with a deafening bang, the sound ringing violently in her ears.

She jolted awake by the desk, a shriek escaping as she leaped up. Her eyes flared with panic, her breath coming in ragged gasps.

She quickly checked her neck and temples, her fingers trembling. Cold sweat trickled down her forehead, causing her fringe to stick in uneven clumps. Her gaze swept left and right, scanning the study as she tried to ground herself, looking for any signs that her nightmare might have been real. The room remained empty and silent, the fears nothing more than the echoes of a restless dream.

She noticed the comforting weight of the jacket draped over her. The lingering scent of tobacco and whisky mingled with the dream's aftermath, stirring a tangle of emotions within her.

Venturing out to the balcony, she found him standing alone, the embers of his smart cigarette glowing softly in the night.

Helix gazed out at the shimmering expanse of Victoria Harbour. He leaned heavily against the stainless-steel railing, a nearly empty glass of whisky dangling from his hand. He turned and saw Bishop by the wide-open balcony doors.

Her arms were folded across her chest, the left one bandaged from the shrapnel wound. His jacket looked oversized draped over her shoulders. Underneath, a grey cotton singlet hugged her curves, the absence of a bra and the soft fabric revealing the natural contour of her breasts. A pair of matching cotton shorts accentuated her hips, and the thick bandage around her thigh still showed dried specks of blood. When his eyes met hers, he saw a troubled look that mirrored his own.

"Why do you always get back so late?" she asked, her voice carrying the soft tremor of someone who had just faced a storm of emotions.

He glanced at her, the shadows of the night obscuring his expression. "Sorry," he replied, "I thought you were already asleep."

"I was. I had a nightmare," she confessed.

Curious, he asked: "Want to share it with me?"

Her response was prompt. "No. Shouldn't you be staying inside? You're exposing yourself to the enemy."

His lips curled into an ironic smile as he stubbed his cigarette. "Right."

They moved back into the apartment and he casually asked, while securing the latches to the French doors: "How's your report progressing?"

Bishop kept her distance, still visibly troubled by thoughts from her nightmare. "It's getting there," she replied. "I need to ask you a few things about Levski and the Cheyevskaya though."

She returned his jacket, feeling its warmth and the lingering scent of him. "Thanks," she said softly.

Her gaze locked with his, and she noted the lightness of his blue irises.

"Anytime. How's your thigh?"

"Better. I can walk somewhat normally now."

"Good," he said, a note of relief in his voice. "I've been worried."

They both paused, feeling the weight of the moment.

"I should head to bed. Do you need me to look at your report right now, or is tomorrow okay?" he began again. "You should go back to sleep too." He placed his hand on her shoulder as he passed her by. "Get a proper rest, remember we have that gala on Friday to worry about."

She caught sight of the strong lines of his back, wondering why he was being so gentle and considerate. Was this part of his game? Was he softening her up to lower her guard? Every instinct screamed at her to stay vigilant, to keep him at arm's length. But the relentless need for human connection, something she had long buried beneath layers of duty and self-discipline, clawed at her resolve.

The tug on his shirt took him aback. Startled, he spun and uttered her name, but she interrupted him.

"Don't go," she whispered. Her hand gripped his arm, not wanting to let go, not wanting to face the night alone. "Stay with me. Just for tonight."

His jaw tightened as he studied her expression, searching those dark brown eyes for whatever secrets she might be guarding. For a brief moment, it looked as if he was about to say something—something that could change everything. But then, to her dismay, he looked away.

"I'm sorry, but I don't think that's a good idea."

Seeing the disappointment flash across her face, he elaborated: "As you said, a close relationship with a fellow agent will not only cloud your judgement and integrity… it also goes against all the virtues *you* believe in. Those rules exist for a reason, right?"

She felt the sting of embarrassment, anger and truth. Doubt gnawed at her, a relentless whisper that made her question who she could trust and what path she should follow.

"Since when are you such a stickler for the rules?" she weakly challenged.

The jibe cut through his resolve. He wrapped his arms around her with a fierce, almost desperate intensity.

"You're making this really hard for me," he said, his voice hushed but sincere.

She could feel the racing of his heart, and the sense of uncertainty mingled with a deep yearning. Her mind screamed of the potential danger she was involving herself in, but she quickly dismissed its warnings. Just for tonight, she wanted to believe in him, to surrender to the promise of connection they shared.

He must have decided to give into it too, for he ran his fingers through her hair, then drove them down to trace the delicate lines of her neck and collarbone.

Anchoring her fingers on his chest, she parted her lips and captured his, moaning softly into his mouth.

Just for tonight.

In that moment, with their bodies pressed together and their emotions laid bare, the boundaries between duty and desire finally blurred, creating a fragile, intimate bond that neither was ready to fully acknowledge or let go.

At first, the kiss was tentative, exploratory, as if they were both testing the waters of something forbidden. Her hands found their way to his nape, feeling the rapid thrum of his heartbeat matching her own.

She felt his hands grip her hips, pulling her closer to him, as he pressed her to the wall. Her breath caught at the feel of the cold hard surface against her back. Nerves, emotions and exhilaration overcame her senses, the kind of adrenaline rush that she normally experienced while on a high-octane mission. This was an erotic dance that built on their banter and sparring sessions, like they were opposing magnetic forces colliding and fighting for dominance.

Her tongue whirled against his while his hands roamed over her body—exploring every curve and touching her in ways that made her giddy with delight and anticipation. Firmly yet gently, he cupped her breast, his thumb grazing the pebbled tip that begged for attention. She arched her back, pressing herself further into his grasp.

His touch was surer now, one hand on her hip, the other caressing the curve of her shoulder, up the lines of her collarbone, and the swell of her rosy cheek. He could feel her body respond to his touch, her hips grinding against him, her desire building within.

She felt the hard ridge of his desire pressed against her thigh. She slid a hand down his torso, her fingers dancing across the taut muscles of his stomach, down the path that led to his treasure trove. Her hand hesitated for a moment, but she knew what she wanted.

She wanted to feel the heat of his body, to stroke every inch of him, including his increasingly rigid length.

The sensation sent a shudder through him, his mind racing with thoughts of her tight, warm embrace. She gazed into his eyes, heart pounding. They were breaking the rules, pushing the boundaries of their relationship, but the need for this release, this moment of scorching flame, was too strong to resist. She deftly unbuttoned his trousers, revealing his arousal, and took it into her hand, feeling him grow even harder in her grasp.

He responded by exerting his dominance, slipping his fingers under her shorts to find her most sensitive spots. To his delight, wetness was already seeping out from her folds. He parted them, exposing her most intimate part, teasing her clitoris and making her buckle against him.

The next few seconds they found themselves busy removing each other's clothing. When all the clothes had been tossed onto the floor, he grabbed her by her backside and lifted her against the cold wall.

Using the wall to prop her up and kissing her wildly, he began thrusting.

She moaned as he entered, the feel of his ample length stretching her insides. She wrapped her legs around his hips for anchor, her heels digging into his glutes as she urged him on, her body begging for more.

Her nails dug into his back, leaving crescent-shaped marks on his flesh. He grunted in reply as he thrust deeper into her depths. Her walls were like a vise grip around him. He couldn't get enough of her warmth, her scent—everything about her was driving him wild. Her moans filled the air around them as they fucked with reckless abandon, like two pieces of puzzle finally fitting into place.

He could feel her breathing becoming more laboured—her body was close to the edge, so close he could taste it himself. He increased his pace even further, each stroke becoming harder, faster, testing the limits of their bodies and pushing them closer to the brink.

Her cries crescendoed as she reached peak. Her body was on fire, every cell within her was screaming for him.

"Alex!"

He rammed her deeper as she rode her wave of orgasm, savouring her burning flesh and the sensation of her hard nipples pressing against his chest. Her hands continued clawing at his back, leaving deep red marks on his skin, but he was too overwhelmed by desire to notice.

When his thighs started to tire, he gradually reduced his speed, using the opportunity to suckle on her silky breasts. In her delirium, she could smell the sweetness of his breath on her skin, and the strong erotic scent that hung in the air. She hung on to his nape and ran her fingers through his hair, messing it terribly.

"Shall we…" he muttered between panting breaths, "move to a bed?"

She could only nod. "Mine."

9 / SCARS

From her vantage point beneath him, she could see his raw power, the way his muscles rippled, the lines on his face contorting, as he lost himself in her.

He was deep inside her again, with protection this time, pounding and thrusting like the relentless barrage of thunder in a storm. The bed creaked as their movements became more aggressive, more forceful, as if they were trying to claim the other with their mark of dominion.

Now that gravity was not working against them, she moved her hips in time to his, matching each thrust and feeling every throb that made her feel alive. She caressed his face, his normally cold visage, now burning with desire to carry them both to the finish. She could not remember the last time she slept with someone with his stamina—she was pretty sure the feeling was mutual.

In that intense moment, as they locked eyes again, he felt the danger of their bond, the potential for betrayal that lurked beyond the veil of lust. No matter—all that mattered was the feel of her lithe body against his and the sight of her dark irises and open lips, beckoning him to never let go.

That proved to be his undoing. He filled her up again and again, brought her over the edge and, in doing so, found his own release. Their bodies trembled with the force of their orgasm, their pleasure echoing through the room.

As they descended from climax, with bodies still entwined and hearts pounding against their chests, they lay breathless and glistening with sweat. She reached out and brushed the hair from his face, her breath still shaky, her hips still trembling from the aftershocks.

He could not bring himself to move, to end this moment.

Softly, he ran his fingers through her skin, stopping at her bandaged thigh. "Was I too rough?"

She chuckled. She was enjoying this feeling too much, of him still being inside her. "No, are *you* hurt?"

He smiled back. "You're the one with the major injury, darling," he replied, checking on the state of her bandaged thigh, and thinking to himself that even when fully healed, the wound was going to leave a nasty scar. He eyed the other faint scars that marred her beautiful body, much like his own battle scars.

They lay in silence, each lost in their own thoughts.

When he finally sat up to clean himself, she could not shake the doubt within—what should she do if he really was a double agent? Honestly, this wasn't the first time she had slept with an enemy, but the chemistry between them, and the fact that she just had the best sex of her life, didn't exactly help.

Her breath hitched as he returned to the bed, his hardness still evident. Whatever doubt had taken root in her mind was overridden by this inexplicable pull he had on her.

She reached out, her hand gliding smoothly over the velvety skin that covered his erection. "How are you still hard?" she coyly asked, looking up at him from the corner of her eye.

He grabbed her by the rear and pulled her close, his fingers tantalisingly close to grazing her nether lips.

"Isn't it obvious?" he purred, enjoying the sight of her squirming at his touch. "You started this."

She felt like wiping the smirk off that handsome face, but had other things to do to him in mind. In one swift motion, she pushed him onto the mattress and got on top of him, letting her breasts hang in full view.

Finally, she thought, *I get to pin you down.*

He wasted no time and began fondling her, her globes fitting perfectly in his palms, while she reached down to massage his scrotum.

In between moans, they exchanged glances, the anxiety coming forth once more, a blend of desire, mistrust, and the looming uncertainty of what lay ahead.

But just for tonight, she'd give in to her deepest desires and fuck him senseless.

Unfortunately, that night turned to day, then turned to night again—and neither of them could take their eyes and hands off each other.

What had started as a shared moment of vulnerability had quickly spiralled into a whirlwind of passion. As the hours melted away, every caress, every touch, became a declaration of their mutual need.

The first night had stretched into day, with fleeting breaks to satisfy basic needs and submitting paperwork—the often overlooked, non-glamorous part of spy work. They also took time to study the details of the upcoming gala, but quickly found themselves back in bed.

In the dead of night, with only light from the open bathroom illuminating their bodies, she was on top of him, resting her head on the side of his chest. Questions of his identity still loomed large in her mind, but she nestled closer to him instead.

"How did you know you wanted to be a spy?" she asked. Throughout the weeks, they had talked briefly about their pasts and fears, but never at this degree of intimacy.

Helix smiled, a distant look in his eyes. "I was twelve. My mother was an embassy attaché, and we were living in Istanbul. I found a hidden compartment in her study. Inside were all these encrypted documents. That's when I realised there was more to her than just being a diplomat. I guess the intrigue hooked me."

She snickered. "Did she know you found her secret stash?"

"Oh, she knew," he said, laughing. "I think she wanted me to find it. She always said I had a knack for touching things I wasn't supposed to." As he said that, he brushed his fingers over her lips, then tucked a stray lock of hair behind her ear. "What about you?"

Her chuckle faded into a smile, her fingers continuing their slow exploration of his taut chest. "My father's a police inspector, and my mum a teacher. I always thought I'd end up either in law enforcement or working with troubled youngsters."

Her face turned sombre. "But then, my brother was killed in a terrorist attack while on a study exchange—in Canada of all places. My parents divorced, I joined the army, the SRR, and finally MI6… I guess I wanted to find his killers, and exact my revenge."

His eyes were sharp. "Did you find them?"

"There was nothing to find, really," she answered poignantly. "It was a splinter cell from a resurgent Keshtan group. The perpetrators were already in custody, and vengeance wouldn't bring Leyton back."

He watched her closely, noting her by-the-book attitude, but also touched by the vulnerability she rarely showed. Pulling her closer, he said: "Have you lost many other people close to you?"

She sighed. "Not personally, but I've had more failed extractions than I'd like to admit," she reminisced. "There was this one operation in Tehran. We were supposed to extract a journalist who had information on a weapons smuggling ring. We were compromised, and she didn't make it out. I still think about her children sometimes."

He nodded, understanding in his eyes. "I had a similar one in Algiers, when I first joined the BND. We were tracking a high-value target, but intel was bad. We walked into a trap, and lost a few good men."

He pointed to the scar running along his ribcage. "I got lucky, it barely missed my lung."

She traced the outline of the scar, her touch gentle but inquisitive. They continued to share their stories, revealing the tales behind each scar, both physical and emotional. It was a strange intimacy, one that brought them closer with each revelation.

He touched a series of faint but raised scars on her wrist, and grew concerned. "And these ones?"

She looked down, a sad smile on her lips. "Those were from when I was a teenager, after my brother died. I was rebellious, got into fights with everyone, and went into deep depression. My parents, even in the midst of divorce, signed me up for therapy. It was a turning point; it made me realise I needed to channel my anger into something productive."

He smiled and kissed the top of her head. "You're one of the toughest people I've met, Luna. And even so… it's OK to admit that we all need help sometimes."

She looked up at him, her heart softening. "What about you, Alex? Have you lost anyone close? What's your biggest fear?"

His gaze darkened slightly. There were secrets, past lives, a failed marriage, that he was tempted to share with her. But he couldn't risk it—not yet.

Instead, he said, cryptically: "In this line of work, we always have to wear masks. Sometimes I fear losing myself in all the deception. Not knowing where the mask ends and I begin."

The answer jolted her as her mind worked over her suspicions. She decided to test the waters.

"Don't tell me you're secretly working for the other side," she pried light-heartedly, monitoring his reaction for the slightest change in demeanour.

His expression didn't change, but the tips of his lips curled up. He got up and easily rolled her onto her back, proceeding to spread her legs, exposing her to him.

"I'm working for one side only: mine," he said with a half-smile. "And right now… I want you," he continued and made his way down to worship her.

She shuddered as he lapped at her nub and began hungrily eating her out. "Alex, I'm still a little sore," she muttered in protest, but her body was betraying her once more, evidenced by her nipples perking up and her juices gradually oozing out and drenching his lips.

"I can be gentle," he promised, appreciating the sight of her heavily lidded almond eyes and her eager flesh quivering at his touch.

He had jokingly called her a moon goddess before, but the analogy seemed very apt. They were like the sun and the moon, always gravitating towards each other in a symphony of light and shadows. Tried as he might, he couldn't resist her, to think clearly, to focus on the mission at hand…

She was a crack in his shining armour, and he wondered if it would be so bad, to not think at all, to find solace in this bond they had forged amidst the chaos.

// Aberdeen Harbour //

The Phoenix Palace was a breathtaking sight, a floating venue that glittered like a jewel against the dark water of Aberdeen Harbour. Small boats scurried back and forth between the pier and the palace, their passengers greeted by the soft hum of the city's nightlife and the occasional flash of camera bulbs.

Tonight's gala, a glitzy affair hosted by the British Consulate General, aimed to raise crucial funds for a seawall project designed to protect Hong Kong's most vulnerable areas. The city's lowlands had become increasingly precarious as rising sea levels threatened their very foundations.

Inside the grand hall, which boasted high ceilings and crystal chandeliers, waiters in crisp uniforms moved gracefully among the guests, offering flutes of champagne and exquisite canapés.

Clarke, dressed impeccably in his formal attire, was stationed at the entrance, warmly greeting each VIP as they arrived. His voice, steady and reassuring, cut through the murmur of excited conversation.

"Welcome, gentlemen," he said, ushering in a group of distinguished-looking men. "Minister Li! How are you?"

"Oh, Mister Clarke! I'm well, thank you for the invitation!" the man responded, his smile as bright as the evening's lights.

"Likewise, Minister Li," Clarke said, his tone amiable. "Let me escort you to Sir Paul," he continued, gesturing toward the foyer. "He has been anticipating your arrival."

As guests mingled and the atmosphere grew increasingly lively, agents stationed around the venue kept a watchful eye, their earpieces crackling with updates.

They were a coordinated team of security personnel tasked to ensure the perimeter's safety. Local police, private security, and intelligence agents teamed up with special ops units, including Helix and Bishop, who had been integrated into the security detail.

"*Are all units standing by?*" came the prompt over the earpieces.

"*Affirmative. We will report unusual movements immediately,*" was the crisp response.

"*Copy that, stay safe,*" came the final instruction.

On the second floor balcony, Bishop was a vision in her flowing gown. The dress, in light blue, cascaded elegantly down her body, the fabric shimmering softly under the chandelier's light. The gown had a fitted bodice that accentuated her figure and a slit that opened just under the garter—where her gun was securely nestled around her good leg.

From her vantage point, she spotted the Dragon Lady arriving by boat. Next to her was Soh, the CIA operative whose presence stirred a mix of curiosity and mystery within her.

As she observed the pair, she caught Helix making his way through the crowd, looking dashing in a classic tuxedo. The sight of him caused a flurry of emotions to surge within her.

When their eyes met, his were both intense and reassuring. He approached her with a purposeful stride. Placing a hand gently on her waist, he whispered, "Don't exert yourself. Your thigh isn't fully healed."

She inhaled his scent, the intimate memories of the past few days flooding her mind. Their recent indulgence weighed heavily on her.

An announcement boomed over the earpieces, drawing everyone's attention.

"*Attention all units,*" the voice stated firmly. "*Our distinguished guest has entered the perimeter.*"

"*Everyone on high alert,*" the directive continued.

Bishop and Helix shifted their eyes to the incoming transfer boat, of which Jiang Yaozu, the Chairman of the Nationalist League, stepped out.

He strode in with an air of undeniable authority. Despite his relatively recent entry into politics, he had quickly risen through the ranks, even becoming the highest-ranking official in the Chinese intelligence agency a few years back. His radical policies had not only won him the recent legislative election but also shaken the global economy. He was hailed as a modern-day figure combining Mao's charisma with Putin's ambition—a formidable candidate for the next leader of the country.

Bishop took a deep breath, looking the man himself in the eye.

10 / PHOENIX AND ASHES

Ten years after the capsizing of Jumbo Floating Restaurant in 2022, a new vessel emerged like a phoenix rising from the waters, its gleaming glass façade reflecting the beauty of Hong Kong skyline at night. The aptly named Phoenix Palace retained Ming grandeur inside, with a grand hall filled with exotic, detailed wooden carvings and rich, red silk drapes.

The distinguished guests had moved from the foyer to the main ballroom, where tables had been set with pristine linens and adorned with fine china. The smell of sumptuous set menus—roasted Peking duck, braised abalones, and fragrant lotus root soup—filled the air as the waitstaff gracefully glided between tables and expertly served dishes, setting them down and serving up.

At one of the central tables, a lively conversation was underway. Sir Paul Young, the British Consul General for Hong Kong, was engaging Jiang.

"Coming back to September, Chairman Jiang," Sir Paul said with a polite smile, "it seems your victory is almost assured, wouldn't you agree?"

Jiang chuckled softly, the corners of his lips curving in a modest grin. "Oh, Sir Paul, you're too kind. While the polls are promising, I'm well aware that other candidates also have a significant chance in the elections."

His accent was American, evidence of an international education. His tone took on a more profound note as he continued. "As for my initial plans for Hong Kong, they are already in motion. I intend to create more job opportunities for local workers."

There was a certain gravity to Jiang's words, his eyes steady and his voice resolute. "To restore Hong Kong entirely to its people," he added, his expression earnest. "This is the noble goal of our Nationalist party."

Sir Paul shifted slightly, Jiang's conviction unsettling him just a little more each day.

Meanwhile, inside and outside the venue, the agents were communicating through a network of radio chatter.

"*Status report, Team One?*" came the call from the control room.

"*Ballroom is stable so far,*" Team One responded.

"*Team Two here,*" followed another update. "*The interior of the restaurant remains normal.*"

"*Balcony, Team Three?*" inquired the control room.

"All good here," Bishop answered from her position on the second floor of the restaurant.

"*Copy that,*" came the acknowledgement.

Her eyes scanned the glittering crowd below. The gala was in full swing, with VIPs and diplomats mingling. Everything seemed under control for now, though her thoughts kept drifting.

She could see Helix pacing around the wooden piers below—part of Team Five. She hated how he could get her heart to flutter just by standing there. She hated that her muscles ached from all their lovemaking, and that she couldn't help feeling like a teenager with a crush during a covert assignment.

He must have sensed that he was being watched, for he spun around and looked up, his eyes meeting hers.

"*What's the matter?*" His voice came through her earpiece through a private line.

"Nothing. Why?" She replied, turning away, while trying to sound nonchalant.

"*You keep looking this way. If I didn't know any better, I'd say you were ogling me.*" She could hear the smirk in his tone.

"You wish," she muttered, rolling her eyes.

Silence.

"*Hey, Luna,*" His voice broke through the private line once more, "*after tonight's assignment… let's have a proper talk.*"

Her heart skipped a beat. What kind of talk? Was he about to declare his love? Making sure that their relationship was nothing more than a physical affair? Or worse still, was he finally confessing that he had been working for the enemy?

She decided to shake off any intrusive thoughts. "If you've got something to say, Alex, just say it now."

He turned to face the water, resting his elbows on a wooden fence, obscuring his expression from her.

"You see, I'm not sure what to make of this… thing between us."

She was about to respond when she noticed his posture change. It was like he saw something—or someone—in the water, that made his nape hair stand.

"Alex?" she leaned into the balcony. "Is everything alright?"

He glanced up at her. *"I'm going to check on something quickly. I'll be right back."*

"Wait, Alex! We're not supposed to leave our posts..."

But he had already disconnected, leaving her with a terrible sinking feeling. Clenching her fists, she made the split-second decision to turn around and head down to the pier. That was when she felt the wall of Julian Soh's chest pressing against her.

She looked up, surprised by his sudden presence.

"Listen carefully, Bishop," he said in a low voice. "Half an hour ago, the Xiao Group heard of a bomb threat. The Dragon Lady decided to still attend the gala to honour Jiang, but we'll leave immediately once any danger appears."

Her heart raced as he continued, "You should tell your team to be on high alert."

Bishop steeled herself. "Thanks for the heads-up, Soh."

"You're welcome," he replied, his eyes remaining on hers for a moment before he moved away. "Be careful."

The grand hall buzzed with energy as the charity auction progressed. Elegant guests in glittering attire gathered around tables, their eyes aimed at the stage.

The auctioneer announced: "Our next lot is a Victorian-era antique drawer made of birch wood. This piece features inlaid oriental-style lacquering. We will start the bidding at 50,000 Hong Kong dollars."

"Ah, 55,000! Thank you, Madam," the auctioneer called out, excitement in his voice. "60,000 to the gentleman in front. Do we have 65,000, 65,000 to combat rising sea levels in Hong Kong lowlands?"

A confident voice rang out from the back, "65,000!"

"Thank you, sir!"

Bishop made her way through the crowd to Clarke, who was seated at a table, observing the proceedings with a keen eye. She leaned in close, her voice low and urgent.

"Clarke, there's something I need to report."

Clarke raised an eyebrow, glancing at the man beside him. "Hmm. Please excuse me, Minister Li." He and Bishop stood and discreetly moved toward a quieter corner.

Back at the auction, the bids continued to rise. "Any further bids? Going once, going twice..."

Soh, who had just returned from his recon, approached the Dragon Lady in one of the VIP tables.

"Miss Xiao," he greeted her.

"Oh, Wan," she acknowledged him with a nod. "How are things outside?"

"Still secure," he assured her. "You need not worry."

Meanwhile, Clarke and Bishop stopped at the grand stairs. Clarke's expression turned stern as he absorbed her information.

"So, it was the CIA agent who informed you?"

"Yes," Bishop confirmed.

"Then prepare the safest evacuation route. And make sure Sir Paul knows nothing of this."

"Yes, sir!" Bishop replied, and took out her phone to scour the best escape routes. But before Clarke returned back inside, she hesitantly added: "Um, Clarke… Helix went outside the perimeter 15 minutes ago and hasn't come back."

Clarke's expression hardened. "Just leave him be. His presence causes nothing but trouble anyway."

Bishop nodded reluctantly, torn between her curiosity and duty as she hurried to implement Clarke's orders.

Further and further away from Phoenix Palace, Helix prowled the fishing piers, his senses on high alert. The night air was thick with just a hint of sea odour, a stark contrast to the festivities inside. Was he seeing things? It felt like he just saw a ghost.

Suddenly, he spotted the flash of red hair again—the unmistakable bob with flailing layers. Vareleva, the Soviet agent he had killed to protect Bishop.

He watched in stunned disbelief as she boarded an empty fishing boat. Determined, he followed her, hop-ping from one boat to the next. Each leap brought him closer, the wooden planks creaking under his weight.

Could it be a trap? He had no choice but to confirm it with his own eyes. As he drew nearer, he saw her hop to yet another boat, but something dropped to the floor with a soft thud.

Bending down, he picked up the discarded item—a wig. *What kind of joke is this?* His eyes darted to a pile of items in the boat's corner, partially covered by a jute cloth. Lifting the cover, his breath caught at the sight of explosives, a significant amount of C4. The timer was already counting down. Five seconds. Four. Three.

No! he thought, lunging away, every muscle tensing as he tried to put as much distance between himself and the impending blast.

Two. One.

The explosion rocked the harbour, sending debris flying and a shockwave that echoed through the night.

Back inside Phoenix Palace, the atmosphere was shattered by the thunderous explosion. The shockwave reverberated through the restaurant, causing glasses to shatter and chandeliers to sway wildly. Gasps turned into screams as panic erupted among the guests.

Bishop's earpiece started blasting with a flurry of queries and shouts between the agents.

"What's happening?"

"A sampan near the pier just exploded!"

The explosion's aftermath was evident even from inside. Smoke billowed, casting an eerie glow as flames licked at the edges of the fishing piers. Before the cause could be determined, another explosion rocked the area—a ferry boat this time.

"*Oh God!*"

"Team Two taking emergency positions. The ballroom is in disarray!"

"Has the Hong Kong sea patrol been informed?"

Bishop's eyes darted around, taking in the scene. Guests were shouting, chairs were overturned, and the once orderly space was now a mess. She spotted Clarke, who was barking orders, trying to restore some semblance of order.

"Protect the VIPs! Tell them help is on the way!" His voice cut through the chaos.

The Dragon Lady turned to Soh, her voice tense but controlled. "Wan?"

Soh, who was talking on the phone, hung up. "Our transport is on its way."

"Then please inform Chairman Jiang to prepare," she ordered.

Outside, the panic was palpable as everyone was scrambling, pushing and shoving in a desperate bid to escape the vessel and return to solid ground. But the transfer boats remained still, and agents had closed off the pier for fear of more threat.

Bishop moved quickly, her eyes tracking the movements of the dignitaries. She led a group of VIPs down the grand staircase while assessing the situation outside. The water was filled with debris from the explosions, making it treacherous to navigate. *How many patrol boats are coming? We can't possibly transfer all the guests in one go,* she thought.

She was also searching for any sign of Helix, wondering if the blast had impacted him…

"You can't board yet, sir! It's still too dangerous on the water!" She overheard a rookie agent trying to fend off guests adamant on entering the transfer boats.

An elegant elderly woman fell and Bishop went over to help her. "Madam, are you alright?"

"I think I've twisted my ankle."

"Let me help you back inside." Bishop said, lifting her with ease.

"No, I need to find my grandson..." The woman's voice was fraught with anxiety, mirroring the fear that gripped everyone.

Suddenly, the guests heard something in the air.

"Help is coming!" someone shouted, a note of hope in their voice.

Bishop furrowed her brows and scanned the horizon. There was no space to land a helicopter here, which meant that it could only be… a seaplane.

The chaos on the floating restaurant reached a fever pitch as the seaplane touched down, its arrival providing a glimmer of hope amidst the turmoil. It was immediately clear, however, that the aircraft was reserved for certain individuals. Bodyguards began to shout over the cacophony, their commands cutting through the panicked crowd.

"Move aside!"

"Make way!"

They hurried Sir Paul Young towards the seaplane, with Chairman Jiang just behind him. Bishop's eyes locked onto Soh and the Dragon Lady, who were also making their way toward the plane amidst the growing turmoil.

Gunfire split the night, sending the crowd into a frenzy of screams and fear. A bodyguard's strained voice rang out, "Jiang has been hit!" followed by urgent commands to protect the Chairman.

Jiang, struck on the side, staggered but managed to stay upright. His aides and bodyguards rushed to his side, struggling to get him on board. When it came to

Dragon Lady's turn to board, Soh caught sight of the sniper perched on the roof. With a decisive shove, he pushed her into the aircraft.

Before he could follow, Soh was hit in the back, his body buckling with the impact. Bishop, who was positioned on the opposite side of the pier, watched the unfolding chaos in stunned silence.

"Wan!" The Dragon Lady's voice was fraught with panic as she reached out to help him, only to be forcibly guided into the plane by her underlings. "Help him up!" she commanded.

The bodyguards quickly complied, lifting Soh and carrying him onto the seaplane. "All VIPs are on board!" one of them announced.

The plane's engines roared to life, the urgency of their escape evident in every movement.

As the seaplane began to ascend, the remaining guests on the floating restaurant turned their attention to the approaching Hong Kong coast guard patrol ships. The sight of the rescue boats coming closer brought a collective sense of reprieve.

"Finally!" someone shouted with relief. "We're safe!" another echoed, their voices a mixture of exhaustion and hope.

The patrol ships worked tirelessly to put out the fires ignited by the explosions, their powerful jets of water cutting through the smoke and debris. Amidst the controlled chaos, a patrol officer approached his captain with a grave report.

"Sir!" the officer called out. "The area has been secured, but we haven't found any physical evidence to begin tracking the suspects."

The captain's brow furrowed. "What did the forensic team uncover?"

The officer shifted nervously. "Forensics detected traces of gunpowder on the top deck of the restaurant. Detectives are interviewing several witnesses, but we don't have anything concrete yet, sir."

The captain's dissatisfaction was evident. "Two people dead, ten injured, and Chairman Jiang goes home with a bullet wound in his side? Who's going to be held accountable for this mess?"

At the pier, the scene was marked by scattered guests wrapped in emergency blankets, their faces etched with shock and cold. Bishop, also wrapped in a blanket, glanced around. She spotted the elderly woman she had helped earlier, who had finally been reunited with her grandson.

"Madam, how is your ankle?" Bishop asked.

"It's better, thank you," the woman replied, her voice trembling slightly.

"That's good to hear," Bishop said. "The patrol ships will return shortly to pick up the last group."

The woman nodded gratefully. "Oh, thank goodness. I was afraid we might be stranded."

As Bishop looked around, her eyes fell on Clarke, who was pacing and talking urgently on the phone. Seeing him in such a state of panic, it was clear that Director Lester wouldn't be the only one demanding answers. And with this incident so glaringly resembling an attempt by the British to undermine Jiang...

Her heart stopped as she noticed a drenched figure sitting alone at the edge of the pier.

Helix was draped in an emergency blanket that hung over his damp form. Soot smeared his face, adding a grim contrast to the scorched remnants of his tuxedo jacket. The singed fabric and the traces of heat on his clothes made it clear he had been close to the explosion. As Bishop's eyes met his, a chill ran down her spine. The sight of him, stark against the surrounding chaos, made her dread the unsettling truth that he had been deeply involved.

11 / AMBUSH

// Admiralty, Hong Kong Island //

The agents gathered in the bowels of SIS Hong Kong station looked weary. It had been hours since they were confined to the briefing room as they tried to make sense of the night's events.

The ergonomic chairs offered little comfort, and though they were provided with food and sustenance, the uncertainty ran them down. Some of them huddled in small groups, exchanging words in low tones. No one dared to ask aloud if this was some form of punishment.

The lack of communication only heightened the anxiety, every minute that passed amplifying the suspicion and fear that things had gone from bad to worse since they left Phoenix Palace.

One of the younger agents let out a heavy sigh and muttered, "That was my first assignment—what a disaster."

A more seasoned operative clapped him on the back, offering a wry smile. "Don't worry, kiddo. There'll be plenty more that'll go even worse than this."

While the others commiserated, Bishop sat on a bench in the corner, her thoughts elsewhere. She couldn't shake her unease at Helix's sudden disappearance and reappearance. She was reminded of the anomalies in his data and activities. Somehow, he always vanished and then showed up at just the right moment.

The door to the room creaked open, drawing everyone's attention. Clarke entered, his expression grim, with Helix close behind. Helix's face was an unreadable mask. He didn't so much as glance at Bishop or the other agents. His hair, now dry, was dishevelled, and his clothes hung on him awkwardly, torn, stained and scorched.

Clarke didn't waste time as he stepped forward to address the team.

"Good morning," Clarke began, his voice cutting, "sorry to keep you all waiting. We've just received updates from the patrol team, as well as from our CIA colleagues. There's good news and bad news."

He paused, allowing the agents to prepare themselves for what was coming. "The good news is that Jiang's condition has been reported as stable. The bullet wound to his side was relatively minor, and all the guests have been safely escorted home. Additionally, the British Consulate is universally viewed as a victim rather than a perpetrator or accomplice of the incident."

The atmosphere in the room lightened ever so slightly, but it was short-lived.

"Now, for the bad news," Clarke continued. "While there were no civilian casualties, last night's incident did claim two lives... including an undercover CIA agent who has been helping us during the gala."

Bishop's heart sank as her thoughts immediately went to Soh. The realisation of his death hit hard.

Clarke pressed on and laid out the grim situation. "So far, Hong Kong police and coast guard have not found any substantial evidence, and the suspect remains unidentified. Given that the Phoenix Palace incident has escalated into an international scandal, Director Lester in London has issued a mandate."

He went through the details, listing the teams one by one, then said: "All agents involved in the operation are required to provide a complete timeline of events. You are to report back here tomorrow morning, except for the sweeper team—you will stay. We are very interested in knowing how a slew of C4 bombs slipped through undetected."

The sweeper agents exchanged weary glances as they faced the daunting task ahead.

Clarke's eyes shifted to Helix, then Bishop. "Special Ops. Since your primary objective in Hong Kong has been partially completed, the Chief of Special Operations wants you both back in London by this afternoon. You're to vacate the safehouse immediately. Any questions?"

No one spoke, orders settling over them like a heavy shroud. Clarke nodded, dismissing them with a simple, "Alright, debriefing over."

As the room began to empty, Bishop sat motionless, her mind swirling with questions about the bizarre scene unfolding before her. *That's it?* she thought, baffled and discouraged. *Why didn't he explain what Helix was doing out there? And what did those two talk about while we were in here for hours?*

The lack of answers only deepened her sense of disorientation, leaving her with a gnawing resolve. She could no longer rely on others to fill in the gaps—she had to uncover the truth herself.

The rideshare had dropped them off in silence, and from the moment they stepped into the apartment, the atmosphere was tense. Not a single word had passed between them during the ride, the quiet stretching uncomfortably.

Helix headed straight for the bathroom, leaving Bishop in a whirl of doubts. The sound of running water soon filled the apartment.

In the shower, he was a silhouette against the frosted glass, the warm water flowing over him in a soothing cascade. Each drop of water that slid down seemed to carry away not just grime but fragments of the explosion. He considered himself lucky to have reached the water fast enough to avoid sustaining any burn.

He stepped out of the shower, towel draped casually over his shoulders as he dried himself. His gaze was distant, his thoughts clearly preoccupied. After slipping into a fresh set of clothes—dark trousers and a fitted shirt that clung to his damp skin—he reached for the hidden compartment beneath the carpet under the bed. With a practised motion, he pried it open, revealing a slim, matte black phone nestled inside. This was no ordinary device; it was his secret line, reserved for only the most critical communications.

He pressed his thumb against the screen, the biometric sensor recognising his fingerprint with a soft click. The phone came to life, its screen illuminating with a new message. As he read it, his jaw clenched, the weight of its contents sinking in.

Tucking the phone back into the compartment, he turned his attention to his gear. He methodically prepared his gun, sliding it into the holster strapped to his back with ease. Next, he fastened his dagger belt around his waist, securing the two tanto blades in their sheaths.

Now he needed to figure out what to do with Bishop.

When he opened his bedroom door minutes later, she was standing in the corridor, the barrel of her SIG aimed directly at him.

"What are you doing?" he asked, coolly.

"Drop your weapons," Bishop demanded, her voice trembling slightly as she gulped.

His expression hardened. "This is not funny, Luna."

"Drop your weapons," she said again, cocking her gun. "Now."

With a heavy sigh, he complied, taking his gun out of the holster and placing it on the floor. Her eyes never left him, tracking his every movement, as she kicked it into the den.

"And your daggers?" she added, tight with mistrust.

He looked away momentarily, frustration giving way to resignation. Reaching behind his back again, he unclipped his dagger belt and threw it in the same direction as his gun.

"Happy now?"

Bishop tightened her jaw, maintaining her stance. "The explosion... that was your doing, wasn't it? And the attempt on Jiang's life..."

He couldn't help but chuckle. "Listen, I don't know where you got that crazy idea—"

"Come on, Helix!" she cut him off, her voice rising. "I took my eyes off you for fifteen minutes, and a sampan had to explode?"

The fact that she reverted to calling him by his codename was not lost on him. He looked her dead in the eye. "This isn't about the sampan exploding, is it?"

The air between them was suffocating, hints of treachery crackling like static electricity.

"And if we're being honest… it's not about what happened tonight, either," he continued.

With a voice strained by the weight of her suspicions, Bishop finally asked the question that had been haunting her for weeks. "Are you really working for Moscow... *Okto*?"

His eyes flickered, just for a moment, but it was enough. Her heart seized, her worst nightmare confirmed.

"How long have you known?" he asked, his tone sharp and icy. Then, with a cruel twist of his lips, he added, "Long enough to seduce me?"

She snapped back, genuinely hurt by the insinuation. "What do you take me for?"

Weariness now etched across his face, he ran a hand through his hair—a tell of his inner turmoil. "Luna, listen—" He reached out to her, but she tightened her grip on the gun, the cold steel digging into her palm.

"Don't." Her voice was hard but tinged with desperation. "Why are you doing this?"

"Why not?" he shrugged, his tone so casually indifferent it made her blood boil. "I'm just taking advantage of a system that's been taking advantage of us."

"Even if it costs the lives of your own colleagues, and country?" she interjected with barely contained fury.

"No king or country gives a damn about us," he snarled, twisted and bitter. "We're just pawns in this game. All that matters is who we can kill and what scraps of intel we can gather for them."

"You think I don't know that?" she fired back. "But nobody forced us to live this life! This is the path we've chosen, and I won't let someone like you abuse it!"

"Oh, really?" His voice dripped with sarcasm, mocking her resolve. "Maybe I should have let Vareleva finish you off that night..."

Before she could react, he lunged at her, knocking her gun across the corridor and locking her neck with his elbow. She used all the strength in her lower body to break free, and brandished her hidden pocket knife in the direction of his torso.

He blinked in shock as she broke away from him, feeling a thin line of blood seeping from a cut across his stomach. The pain was sharp, but the sight of her fierce, seething anger was more pressing. She growled with a primal rage and lunged toward her gun, determined to reclaim it.

In a rare lapse of control, he lost his temper entirely and hurled himself at her. The impact sent the both of them crashing to the floor. As they tumbled together, he managed to pin her down, his hands closing around her throat with a fierce, unyielding grip.

Bishop's body writhed beneath him, her limbs flailing with frantic energy. She tried to break free, aiming sharp kicks and using her agility to twist and squirm beneath him. But he countered with his true strength, shifting his weight to block her movements, his body pressing down with an oppressive force.

Her hands clawed desperately at his, nails biting into skin in a futile attempt to pry his fingers away. Her vision tunnelled as the pressure on her throat became unbearable and a cold wave of panic surged through her, threatening to drown her in helplessness.

"I… trusted you…" she gasped, choking out from deep within her lungs.

The rage in his eyes began to waver, his grip loosening incrementally as she gasped for air. He shifted his weight, lowering himself closer to her, his hands moving to pin her arms above her head. His harsh whisper cut through the space between them.

"How have you survived this long as a spy, with that naivete of yours? It's infuriating."

His reprimand was sharp, but the ferocity of his touch had faded, revealing the inner conflict eating at him. The heat of their bodies pressed together created an unsettling intimacy that underscored the volatility in their partnership.

This distraction gave Bishop the opening she needed. She kneed him hard just above his groin, causing him to buckle immediately.

"Fuck you, Helix!" she shouted, watching him recoil in pain. "I told you not to patronise me!"

With pain still etched across his face, his expression shifted abruptly to cold focus. He held up a hand, the military signal to halt, and then, wincing, he tapped his ear, pointing toward the door—intruders. The sound of approaching footsteps triggered a familiar rush in Bishop's chest.

Helix quickly grabbed her gun and tossed it back at her, gesturing urgently toward her room. Despite her simmering resentment, her instinct for survival, honed by years in the field, took over.

As he barely rolled to his feet, a barrage of bullets erupted, shattering the silence. Wood splintered from the sliding door, raining down the hallway. She sprang into her room while he dove into the den.

Scrambling to her feet, Bishop grabbed a magazine from a drawer and reloaded. The corridor filled with another volley of bullets and the sharp sounds of Russian voices, fast and clipped. Her mind raced with questions: What was happening? Who were they targeting? But there was no time for answers—survival was all that mattered.

She raised herself just enough to peek around the open door, firing a few shots through the hallway with deadly accuracy. Helix, now with his gun back, did the same, and together they managed to gun down some of the intruders. She could hear the return fire, the Russian commands, and the pounding of boots as the attackers tried to breach their defences.

With the smoothness of a trained operative, Helix darted through the chaos, flinging open the door to his room to get more ammo. But a movement from Bishop's room caught his eye—agents on ropes, descending fast toward the high-rise window.

"Window!" he shouted, his voice cutting through the din.

She threw herself behind the heavy armoire just as the window shattered, the room exploding into a storm of glass shards and chaos. The first attacker swung in, boots hitting the floor with a thud, her gun already sweeping the room. Helix, from his position in the doorway, fired in quick succession, the deafening blasts echoing. His first shot hit true, dropping the lead agent mid-step.

Another agent returned fire with a brutal consequence. The large round tore through Helix's left shoulder, ripping a hole through flesh and bone. The force knocked him off his feet, slamming him into the floor.

"Helix!" Bishop screamed. She squeezed off two shots, both hitting home as the intruders collapsed. Her focus sharpened to a razor's edge as she reloaded and pivoted to the hallway, where more agents had stormed in. She fired again and again, each pull of the trigger sending another adversary crumpling to the ground.

As her gun clicked empty, she realised with a sickening jolt that one attacker was still standing. He stepped into her room, his gun levelled, ready to end it.

The blade spun through the air, finding its target. The agent staggered, eyes wide in shock, before crumpling to the ground, the dagger buried deep in his throat.

Bishop's heart pounded as she traced the weapon's trajectory to its source. There lay Helix, sprawled on the floor, his half-empty dagger belt beside him, blood beginning to spread across the carpet of his room.

She rushed to his side after confirming the area was secure. His shirt was soaked with blood, revealing a jagged hole in his shoulder—too severe for her to manage alone. Every instinct urged her to call for a medic or find help immediately.

She heaved him up with all her strength, propping him against the side of the bed. Stripping off her sports jacket, she pressed it against the wound in a desperate attempt to stem the bleeding, but the blood continued to seep through.

Half-conscious, he gripped her arm, his voice strained but firm. "Go," he rasped, "more will be coming."

Who even are they? Her mind screamed in confusion. "Then we need to get back to the consulate!" she insisted.

His response was a pained, almost mocking smile. "So you can hand me over to Clarke?"

"What?" she snapped, bewildered. "No, I haven't even told them you're working for the enemy..."

He cut her off, his voice growing weaker. "Save yourself. I won't last long with this shoulder."

"You'd rather die here??" Her exasperation boiled over in disbelief.

"Maybe it's for the best," he murmured, his breath shallow. "Clarke will kill me anyway…" The resigned smile returned.

"FINE!" she finally retorted, her anger mixing with desperation. "I'm not wasting any more time trying to follow that twisted logic of yours!"

She stormed out of the room, heading into hers to grab more ammo and a fresh jacket. Pressing her back against the wall, she cursed under her breath. She had seen enough battlefield injuries to know that this one was bad—really bad. Helix was hanging on by a thread, and the odds of him making it were slim at best.

She pulled out her phone, grappling with her next move.

When she returned to his side, she found him staring up at her, his eyes clouded with pain.

"You're still here?" he croaked, his voice barely audible.

"Yeah," she replied, determination settling over her. "I'm getting you out of here." Part of her wanted to leave him behind, to let him pay for the secrets and lies. But another part of her, the part that had seen the man beneath the double agent, couldn't abandon him.

She quickly fashioned another makeshift bandage for his shoulder and draped a coat over him. "Don't get the wrong idea," she said, "I'm not letting you die before you explain everything."

Slipping her arm under his, she lifted him to his feet, taking on most of his weight. Every step was a battle, but she pushed forward. The hallway reeked of gunpowder and sweat, mingling with the acrid stench of blood and smoke. It was eerily silent, littered with fallen bodies and the chaotic aftermath of their fight. The only sounds were the distant wail of sirens and their ragged breaths.

As they stumbled toward the lift, his grip on consciousness kept fading, his breaths coming in short, painful gasps. She wrapped her arm around his waist, half-carrying and half-dragging him.

Bishop kept her focus on the task at hand. The fight wasn't over, and they were still alive. And as long as she had breath in her body, she would keep fighting.

12 / THE FIFTH COLUMN

In the oppressive darkness of his unconscious mind, he found himself transported back to Munich of a few years ago. The memory was vivid, each detail etched deeply into his psyche.

The argument with Anna had reached its peak.

Their fights always circled back to the same issues: his constant absences and the secrets that came with the life of being a soldier and—later—spy. The missions pulled him away for weeks, sometimes months, leaving her to navigate life on her own. Even when he was home, the walls he'd built around his work were impenetrable. She craved honesty and openness, someone who could truly share a life with her. But with him, it felt like she was living with a shadow, a man who was there but never really present.

She stood by the window, her back turned to him as tears slid down her face.

"I can't do this anymore, Alex," she said, speaking German, her voice trembling. "I'm so tired of the secrets, the lies… the constant fear of what you're not telling me."

He couldn't give her a satisfactory answer. This was the life he had become embroiled with, and he couldn't risk bringing his family into danger, no matter how much he loved them—precisely because he loved them.

As he stayed silent, Anna spoke again, in between soft sobs, "See? Every time we argue, you just shut down. It's like you don't even see me."

He had seen her cry countless times, usually because she believed—erroneously—that he no longer cared. But this time, it felt final. He wondered if their bond had finally become too broken to fix.

"Papa?"

Their son appeared in the hallway, a small figure silhouetted against the dim light.

His eyes widened, but he tried to mask his pain with a gentle tone. Kneeling down, he tousled the boy's hair. "Lukas, what are you doing up?"

Lukas, barely three, rubbed his eyes. He peeked into the master bedroom, where Anna was wiping her tears with the back of her hand, trying to compose herself.

"Mama, are you OK?"

"She is, sweetheart," he quickly replied, leading Lukas away from the master bedroom. "Come on, I'll take you back to bed and put your music box back on."

He carried Lukas over his shoulder, but the boy kept staring in the direction of the bedroom. "Papa?"

"Yes?"

"Mama always gets sad when you go to work."

His heart ached at the innocent observation. Hiding his tears, he assured him: "I know, but it'll be fine, Lukas. As long as Mama has you, she'll be fine."

That night, as he watched his son drift back to sleep, his heart shattered into pieces. He felt utterly powerless as Anna eventually left, taking Lukas with her, their departure leaving an unfillable void.

Each memory of them was a ghost he tried to push aside as he faced the dangers of his perilous life, almost as if he were daring death to claim him. Months blurred into years, but the question remained, haunting him: why did he keep going?

The sun hung high in the sky, the air filled with the faint scent of antiseptic. Helix's eyelids fluttered, and he groaned softly as he came to. His left shoulder throbbed with sharp, jagged pains. He felt sick and disoriented, unsure of who or where he was.

Bishop sat in a worn chair beside the bed, her head resting on her arms, which were crossed on the edge of the mattress. She was half asleep, with dark circles under her eyes, a tanktop stained with dried blood, and a still bandaged left arm.

His voice was a whisper. "Luna."

Her head snapped up, eyes suddenly alert as she saw him awake. "Helix," she reached out to touch his forehead, checking for a fever. "You're awake. Thank God."

He tried to sit up, wincing at the pain. His torso was bare save for the tight bandage that wrapped around his chest and shoulder. It was stained with blood—some of it had dried into a dark, rusty hue, while fresh, crimson blotches still seeped from the hole at his shoulder.

"Take it easy," she said, her tone firm yet gentle as she helped him to a half-seated position against the wall, placing a pillow behind him. She began preparing another dose of painkiller. "I can't give you too much for fear of making you pass out again. So, bear with the pain a bit, alright?"

He let her inject the syringe into his vein, noting the ampoules of medical-grade painkillers on the nightstand. He tried to gather his thoughts while scanning the dingy small room. "Where are we?"

"Chungking Mansions," she replied. "You've been out for two days. You lost a lot of blood, but the large round didn't hit any arteries. This place isn't short of illegal yet competent doctors either. In short… you got lucky."

He looked at her, wondering why she had brought him here instead of handing him over to Clarke. She looked tired; perhaps just as tired as he was.

Her next move was to give him some soft cookies and water, which he accepted and ate in silence.

As the morphine-fentanyl mix began to course through his veins, he felt the pain gradually ebb away. His thoughts grew hazier in exchange, but it wasn't a bad trade-off.

"Thank you," he finally murmured, "for bringing me here… and not letting me die."

She didn't answer, but sat back in her chair, eyes piercing despite the fatigue.

"If you really want to thank me… start talking."

Fully leaning back on his pillow, he managed a small, wry smile. *Fine.* "What do you want to know?"

"How long have you been working for Moscow?" was her first question.

"Almost five years," he admitted warily. "Since '31."

Her eyebrows knitted together. "Back when you were still with the BND?"

"Yes," he confirmed. When she shot him a questioning look, he closed his eyes and continued, "I was stationed in Amsterdam and ran into an old friend from the military college. We went to a local pub to catch up, and the conversation flowed with the drinks."

He explained that his friend, also a BND agent then, was frustrated with the agency, feeling the danger far outweighed the pay. Half-jokingly, the friend mentioned having contacts on the Soviet side.

"He invited me to join him, promising that the pay would be twice the risk."

Bishop let out a small snort. "Funny. I didn't peg you for the type easily motivated by money."

Helix clarified, "It wasn't about the money. I was younger then. Young, and filled with rage."

He described how, as a trainee operative, his team was frequently sent on high-risk missions, only to be abandoned while the more experienced second team swooped in to neutralise the enemy.

"We lost so many young recruits through that extreme screening process, and the trauma never left me."

Bishop's expression softened, though she kept her guard up. "I didn't realise you had feelings," she said, immediately wondering if she'd gone too far.

"There's a lot you don't know about me," he replied matter-of-factly.

The silence that followed was charged, almost magnetic. She averted her gaze, trying to recentre as fatigue began to weigh on her.

"Who's pulling your strings as Okto?" she asked, continuing the interrogation.

"A Sluzhba official named Stoklitsky, though that doesn't matter anymore."

Bishop frowned. "Why not?" she pressed, the memory of the bloody ambush at the apartment flashing through her mind. "If you're really working for the Soviets, why did they send troops to kill you?"

Helix remained silent for a moment before shaking his head. "I can't tell you. You're better off not knowing."

In an instant, she was on her feet, her hand slamming against the mattress. The sudden force made both him and the bed jolt. "Are you fucking joking?" she snapped. "It's too late to say that now! After everything that's happened, don't I deserve the truth? Huh, Helix?"

He let out a long sigh, the weight of secrets pressing down on him. They locked eyes, a clash of wills, before he spoke again.

"Have you ever heard of пятая колонна?"

She blinked at the Russian phrase. "*Pyataya kolonna*—The Fifth Column?"

He nodded. "Yes, the Fifth Column is a secretive division within the Sluzhba, created by a few powerful officials in Moscow. Even within their own ranks, it's controversial."

"How so?"

His eyes searched hers for understanding. "Think about it, Luna. What does Moscow think of Jiang?"

"Jiang?" she echoed, thinking back. "He's always been a radical populist, a huge threat to the stability of the Red Pact."

"Exactly," Helix agreed, "so if you're the Soviets, what do you do? The Fifth Column acts like a hidden pillar within their structure, ensuring the Red Pact endures for Neo-Soviet prosperity. The best way to do that is to prevent someone like Jiang from gaining power."

He paused, letting the implication sink in before adding, "But everything has to be done cleanly. The best way is to use Allied operatives to spy on Beijing. That way, both the Soviets and us benefit…"

Bishop's eyes widened in realisation. "Is that why you've always been so successful in your missions in China? Because the Soviets leaked information to you to undermine Chinese nationalists?"

"As long as it aligned with their goals, the safety and missions of the fifth columnists were a priority," Helix confirmed.

Bishop thought, *A network of Western operatives secretly on the Neo-Soviet payroll, spying on Chinese nationalists.* The craziest part? Somehow, it didn't even seem to hurt the Allies.

"Then why did they turn on you?" she pressed, confusion lacing her voice. "Surely not because you failed to kill Jiang?"

Helix shook his head, a grim smile on his lips. "I don't know why you keep linking me to Jiang's shooting. I told you, I didn't do it. I was chasing someone who looked like Vareleva. By the time I realised it was a setup, I was in a sampan rigged with explosives…"

"It was all a trap?" Bishop asked, incredulous. "Then who's the real culprit?"

"I'm still not sure," he admitted. "The Soviets might have had a motive to eliminate Jiang, but their methods are rarely that direct."

"So why were they after you?" she demanded.

His expression darkened. "Because the Fifth Column has been disbanded. Our operations weren't effective anymore. Assets were being lost left and right, not to mention all the Soviet agents assigned to protect us. The Sluzhba station chiefs in China convinced Moscow to eliminate the Fifth Column entirely. And now... here we are."

Bishop's thoughts spiralled, absorbing the enormity of Helix's revelations. The Soviets not only created and then dismantled a secret division but also hunted down their own operatives? The idea was chilling.

"Abandoning assets is one thing," she said, her voice tight, "but actively murdering them? These are the people you chose to work for?"

Helix gave her a faint smile. "No, you're forgetting something important, Luna. I killed Vareleva and some of her men. With the Fifth Column gone, Kuznetsov now has free rein to come after me—after us."

Bishop's heart sank at his words, and the realisation hit her like a cold wave. That was the other question that had been haunting her, that burned above all else in her mind.

"Why did you kill Vareleva?" she finally dared to ask. "That night, why didn't you let her kill me?"

His eyes flickered, a shadow of reluctance crossing his pale face. He looked away, unable to meet her gaze.

Her heart pounded as she watched him struggle with his emotions. "Tell me," she insisted, her voice trembling slightly. "I need to know."

He cleared his throat, searching for the right words. "Honestly? You infuriate me. A lot. We've clashed and been at odds more times than I can count. But…"

The harsh edges of his voice softened as he continued, "I'm envious of your idealism. Your belief in what's right reminds me of how I used to be, how I once thought I could take on the system and change it."

He shifted closer, his voice dropping to a more intimate murmur. "I feel drawn to you. It's like a pull, a burning flame that I can't ignore." His eyes traced the contours of her worn face, the curve of her lips, the way her raw beauty seemed to intoxicate him at every turn.

Her cheeks burned as he leaned in to caress her face, his eyes intense and smouldering. "This is more than just lust, Luna—you know that. You drive me to the edge. Everything about you: the way you think, the way you move, the way you look at me—it creates this deep, almost desperate need to be close to you, to protect you, to be a part of your world…"

The admission hung in the air, gut-wrenching and poignant. The intensity of his feelings left them both touched and unsettled. Her breath caught in her throat as her eyes welled up.

That was when the crackle of a radio transmission reached their ears, its static echoing from outside the door.

The special unit of agents had assembled on the ground floor of Chungking Mansions. The team leader, clad in tactical gear, addressed his unit with a hush.

"Targets identified as Shadow and Striker. No mistakes. We go in, neutralise, and extract."

The agents nodded in unison. They moved with practised efficiency, their footsteps almost silent on the worn tiles. The leader signalled for the group to split, half taking the stairs while the others took the elevator, their weapons at the ready.

As they ascended, their radios crackled with updates. "Team Alpha in position. We are on floor five."

"Copy that, Team Bravo approaching from the east corridor."

Back in the room, Bishop's ears pricked up at the sound of footsteps and the crackle of radio chatter echoing down the corridor from both directions. She pulled away slightly.

Helix didn't hesitate. "You need to go, now!" he urged, his voice low but insistent. Darting his eyes at the half-broken window, he ordered: "Leave me one sidearm. Climb out the window and head into the courtyard!"

But she remained rooted to the spot, shaking her head as she placed a hand on his chest.

He stared at her, exasperated and confused.

She trembled, tears spilling down her cheeks as she felt the thrum of his heartbeat beneath her palm. "I'm sorry, Alex. Those aren't Soviet agents outside."

His eyes widened, a flash of understanding dawning as she continued, her voice cracking. "When I contacted Snatch this morning, he told me the MI6 higher-ups already know you're working for Moscow. After the ambush, and because you disappeared… they named you the primary suspect in Jiang's shooting."

She struggled to keep going, biting her lip to hold back the sobs. "And since I was nowhere to be found..."

He gently finished for her, "They thought you were involved too."

She nodded, tears falling freely now.

"I understand," he whispered, a bittersweet smile tugging at his lips. "You did what you had to…"

Before the crushing reality of their situation could overwhelm them, he pushed off the bed and pulled her into a desperate kiss.

The moment their lips met, it was as if time itself had stopped. A torrent of emotion surged through her, setting her heart ablaze. The kiss was fierce, filled with all the words they couldn't say, all the fears they couldn't face. Her pulse thundered in her ears, drowning out everything but the feel of him—his warmth, his touch, the way his heartbeat echoed her own. Every doubt, every fear melted away as she clung to him, pouring everything she had into that single, searing instant, knowing it might be their last.

Just as quickly as it had begun, the moment was shattered.

The door burst open with a crash, and a flood of agents stormed in, weapons ready to fire, shouts slicing through the air like knives.

"Hands where we can see them! Down on the ground, now!" the team leader barked.

Bishop pulled back, her heart still racing, her breath ragged. Helix's hand lingered on her cheek for a split second before he let go, his expression stoic as he turned to face the intruders.

The agents moved in and brutally restrained them, methodically seizing all weapons and incriminating objects. She watched helplessly as they manhandled Helix, his body sagging under the weight of his injuries.

"Be careful with him!" Her voice broke through the chaos, desperate and raw. "He needs medical attention!"

Pain exploded as one of the agents delivered a hard blow to the back of her neck. Her vision blurred, she fell to the floor, her body going limp. Just before the world turned black, she turned her gaze to Helix. Their eyes met for a fleeting second, and in his weary blue eyes, she saw a mix of regret, sorrow, and something she couldn't quite place. Hope, perhaps.

"Forgive me..." she managed to whisper, her voice a mere breath, before the darkness swallowed her whole.

// Islington //

It was anything but a typical July day. The steady rhythm of raindrops drummed against the window panes, casting an almost hypnotic spell over the city. Snatch sat in his home office, the glow of his holoscreen illuminating his expression as he lost himself in the chaos of an online multiplayer game. His fingers danced across the laser keyboard, his concentration unbreakable—until a flicker on his security system drew his attention.

"AFK," he quickly typed to his teammates, his mind already shifting gears. He leaned closer to the screen, scanning the live feed. A sense of rush gripped him as he bolted to the door, a storm of questions and emotions brewing inside him.

As he opened the door, she stood there, looking up at him with those familiar dark brown eyes.

"Luna," he breathed, eyes widening in disbelief.

She stood in the rain, an umbrella shielding her from the downpour. Her hair was shorter now, cut into a layered bob. Despite the rain and the sombre atmosphere, she wore a smile on her face.

"Hi, Rob," she said softly, "long time no see."

13 / RAIN IN SUMMER

SIS AI Cloud / ORION
INTERROGATION REPORT: 'Bishop' / Special Ops

Security Clearance: Level 5
Report date: July 28, 2036

COMMITTEE MEMBERS

Director of Secret Intelligence Service, Chief Legal Officer, Chief of Special Operations, Deputy Director of Counterintelligence, Chief of Personnel Affairs

BACKGROUND

Following the Phoenix Palace incident (PPI) and the subsequent shooting of Jiang Yaozu, operative 'Bishop' and senior operative 'Helix' of the Special Operations Division were apprehended by SIS operatives. Due to Helix's suspected double agent status and the chaotic nature of events surrounding the shooting,

Bishop was placed under intense scrutiny. The following report outlines the findings from her interrogation and the committee's decision regarding her role within the SIS.

INTERROGATION SUMMARY

Knowledge of Helix's Activities

Bishop confirmed that she had limited knowledge of Helix's activities, particularly his involvement with the 'Fifth Column' and his interactions with Neo-Soviet operatives. The only information she possessed was what Helix voluntarily shared with her when she confronted him after PPI.

Disappearance after Safehouse Ambush

Bishop admitted to disappearing for several days after the ambush at her Hong Kong safehouse. She made the decision to take the severely wounded Helix into hiding rather than turn him over to authorities, driven by a belief that Helix was not involved in PPI. She emphasised that her actions were intended to gather information from Helix, not to abet any unlawful activities.

Involvement in Jiang Shooting

Bishop denied any involvement in the shooting of Jiang during PPI. The evidence corroborates her claim, as no direct or indirect ties were found linking her to the incident.

Awareness of Fifth Column Activities

Bishop's awareness of the Fifth Column and their activities was minimal. She understood them as a rogue element within the SVR, but lacked specific details. Her knowledge was primarily shaped by Helix's brief mentions, and she did not play an active role in their operations.

Failure to Report Helix's Double Agency

The primary concern identified during the interrogation was Bishop's failure to report Helix's potential double agency when she first became suspicious. While she acknowledged that there were moments of doubt, she deliberately chose not to inform her superiors or report her findings to ORION. This was identified as a significant lapse in judgement, but one motivated by her assessment of the circumstances rather than willful disobedience.

Relationship with Helix

The committee noted a close bond between Bishop and Helix, which appeared to be more than professional in nature. This bond likely influenced Bishop's decisions, particularly her choice to protect Helix after the ambush. The committee expressed concern that this relationship could compromise Bishop's objectivity and effectiveness in future operations.

COMMITTEE DECISION

After reviewing the evidence and statements from both Bishop and Helix, the committee has reached the following conclusions and decisions:

Exoneration from Major Offences

Bishop is exonerated from any involvement in the shooting of Jiang, PPI, and the double agent activities of Helix. The committee finds no evidence to suggest that Bishop was complicit in these events.

Formal Reprimand

While Bishop is cleared of major offences, her failure to report suspicions regarding Helix's double agency constitutes a breach of protocol. A formal reprimand will be placed on her record, highlighting the importance of reporting all potential threats to the Crown, regardless of personal relationships or uncertainties.

Suspension Followed by Reinstatement with Restrictions

Bishop is to undergo a three-month suspension period, after which she will be reinstated to her role within the SIS. However, her activities will be closely monitored for a probationary period of six months.

Severance of Contact with Helix

The committee strongly advises that Bishop sever all personal and professional contact with Helix upon her release. The potential for conflict of interest and compromised judgement is deemed too high, and any further communication with Helix will be considered a breach of SIS protocol.

Mandatory Counselling

Bishop will be required to attend mandatory counselling sessions to address the emotional and psychological impacts of the recent events, with a focus on maintaining professional boundaries and decision-making under pressure.

CONCLUSION

The committee recognises Bishop's loyalty and dedication to her duties, while also acknowledging the mistakes made in the heat of a complex and emotionally charged situation. The decisions outlined aim to balance accountability with the potential for Bishop's future contributions to the SIS.

Signed:

- Director of Secret Intelligence Service
- Chief Legal Officer
- Chief of Special Operations
- Deputy Director of Counterintelligence
- Chief of Personnel Affairs

End of Report
ORION Reference Code: IR-28072036-Bishop

// Leicester Square //

Snatch and Bishop sat across from each other in a cosy Sichuan restaurant at the edge of Chinatown. The place was buzzing with activity, the scent of sizzling dishes in the air. They had just finished their meals, and now, with a moment of quiet between them, Snatch leaned back in his chair, casually starting the conversation.

"When did you get out of detainment?" he asked, his tone light but laced with genuine concern.

"Two days ago," Bishop replied, taking a sip of her tea. "The moment I got home, I found the roof leaking all over the place."

Snatch chuckled, shaking his head. "This summer's been real strange, hasn't it?" His eyes drifted to her hair, which was noticeably shorter than before. "Why did you decide to cut your hair? Though, I have to say, it suits you."

Bishop absently ran her fingers through her cropped hair. "Yeah, my hair got all messed up after detainment. Plus, I was anticipating a much hotter summer."

Concern flashed across Snatch's face. "What did they do to you in there, Luna?"

She exhaled, her gaze dropping to the table as memories of the cold briefing room resurfaced. The days had blurred together, each one marked by relentless interrogations. They didn't resort to physical violence, but the pressure was suffocating. Every session felt like a mental battle. They hurled questions at her, demanding to know her involvement in the Phoenix Palace incident, her connection to Helix, and her loyalty to her country.

But she played it down, explaining: “I was interrogated over and over, and in the end, they proved I wasn’t involved at all. They confiscated my weapon and suspended me for three months. It could’ve been worse, I suppose. Compared to what Helix is going through…”

Her thoughts drifted to Helix, a mix of sadness and something deeper weighing down her heart. She pictured him in a cell much like hers was, bruised and bloodied, but still defiant.

“Hey, Snatch,” she said, snapping back to the present. “Any updates on the Jiang shooting?”

Snatch reached for his phone, his fingers scrolling through his Orion feed. “Not much yet. MI6 has formed a special commission to track down the suspect, with increasing pressure from the Chinese side.”

He showed her the screen, a series of images and internal memos flicking by. “In the meantime, Director Lester is trying to neutralise media coverage, and Chief Adamson’s been asked to clarify things as well.”

Bishop scanned the feed, her thoughts drifting to Adamson. Helix had always been her favourite agent. What was the Chief's reaction to all this?

"Snatch," she asked, her voice tinged with worry. "Did they find a lot of evidence that incriminates Helix?"

Snatch took back his phone, his expression sombre. "Not really. The investigators have delved into every detail of his life and visited all of his listed addresses in the UK and Europe, but it looks like all those places have been recently… 'cleaned'."

"'Cleaned?'" Bishop repeated, her brow furrowing. "You mean, like what happened to our apartment in Hong Kong?"

"Huh?" Snatch looked puzzled.

Bishop explained, "While I was in detainment, I was told the safehouse in Hong Kong was found empty. There were bullet casings and bloodstains, but no bodies were left behind. And all the data we collected during the mission—gone."

Snatch muttered under his breath, "Those Guoanbu agents move fast, don't they?"

Bishop's confusion deepened. "Guoanbu? Snatch, it wasn't the Chinese who ambushed us—it was the Soviets! This was all orchestrated by Kuznetsov…"

At that moment, a waiter approached their table. "Excuse me sir, you asked for the bill?"

Snatch nodded, "Do you have the machine?" He reached for his wallet.

Bishop protested. "Rob, isn't this my treat?"

"You can get the next one," he said with a smile, waving her off. "I'm a regular here, and I get a discount."

As the waiter left, Snatch leaned in, his voice dropping to a whisper. "Hey, what do you mean it wasn't the Chinese who ambushed you? How could the Soviets have gone after Helix?"

Bishop looked at him, worried. "You don't know about this? Helix was black-flagged by the Soviets. His handler in Moscow abandoned him, and Kuznetsov—the station chief—was hunting him down because he killed their agents!"

Snatch's eyes widened in surprise. "So, that ambush had nothing to do with the Jiang shooting?"

"I don't know," Bishop admitted, her voice filled with uncertainty. "It's possible Moscow knew that Helix was a suspect in the Jiang case. If that's true… then they had even more reason to eliminate him before their connection was exposed, right?"

Why isn't any of this information on Orion? she wondered, feeling that something was off. Just as she was about to voice her concerns, Snatch interrupted.

"Luna," he said, his eyes locking onto hers. "Do you trust this man?"

She hesitated, her mind racing. "I have to. After everything he's done for me…"

"That's not a reason!" Snatch's voice was sharp, his frustration breaking through.

Before Bishop could respond, the waiter returned with the card machine. The moment passed, dread hanging in the air as she sat quietly, her thoughts still tangled in the complicated web surrounding Helix.

They walked from Chinatown back to her house in Whitechapel in a light drizzle, Bishop under her umbrella and Snatch tucked into his water-repellent hoodie. The wet pavement shimmered under the dim streetlights. After a few moments of silence, Bishop broke it.

"Snatch," she began hesitantly, "if I may, I actually need a favour."

He glanced at her, sensing the seriousness in her tone.

"I still have access to Orion during suspension, but it's very restricted. I was wondering if you could give me access to the MI6 intelligence database and those of our allies," she continued. "I need to find out what really happened in Hong Kong..."

Snatch stopped in his tracks, the colour draining from his face.

"You're joking, right?" His voice was bordering on anger. "Do you have any idea how complicated your situation is right now? Jiang's shooting has impacted UK-China relations and become a black stain on MI6's history. Now that you're free, you want to dig it all up again?"

When she looked at him with defiant eyes, his resentment boiled over. "Did you know? When you were hiding Helix in Kowloon, every Allied agent was sent out to hunt you down like wild dogs! Considering the magnitude of the Phoenix incident and the fact that you were aiding a double agent, you're lucky they let you go as quickly as they did!"

His words cut through the rain-soaked night. Bishop didn't respond, but stopped walking just a few metres from her front door. Snatch took a deep breath, his tone softening as he spoke again.

"Listen, Luna," he said, his voice calmer, "in our profession, sometimes it's what we don't know that keeps us alive. Just lie low for now, OK?"

She finally spoke, her voice full of remorse. "I'm sorry, Snatch. Every time I act recklessly and irrationally, you're the one who always helps me find a way out. Even now, while I'm being punished for my selfishness, you're still here, accepting me, and I truly appreciate that. But..."

She paused as she felt the rain stop, closing her umbrella and shaking it dry. "I know Helix didn't pull the trigger that hit Jiang. And the mysterious handling of this case only makes me more certain of his innocence."

She stepped closer to her front door, taking out her keys. "I don't know what I'm looking for, and I'm not sure I'll find it, but... if we were the ones in that position, wouldn't we fight to help each other?" She turned back to face him, her expression firm.

Snatch looked at her, the resolve in her eyes convincing him, albeit reluctantly.

"Well, if you put it that way, how can I refuse?" he sighed, conceding. "Alright, I'll help you as much as I can, BUT! The moment you start acting out of line, I'll pull the plug on everything. Understood?"

Bishop smiled, the tension in her features easing. "Yes, sir!"

She leaned over, gratitude evident in her eyes. "Thank you, Rob. I don't know what I'd do without you..."

She gave him a quick peck on the cheek and disappeared inside, leaving Snatch standing on the porch, a bit dumbfounded.

He blinked, staring at the closed door, thinking to himself why he hadn't been invited in.

He chuckled disappointingly under his breath, shaking his head. What a sweet talker she was. It had always been one of her strengths, weaving her charm into situations to get what she wanted. And he, despite everything, found himself caught in her web once again.

He looked up at the clearing night sky, thinking how things had just become more complicated, but he should probably just go with the flow…

In the MI6 office, Snatch sat at his cubicle, lost in thought. The gentle hum of the air conditioning and constant feed of data arriving on his screens created a tranquil backdrop. His mind was elsewhere, pondering over the latest developments.

The sudden tap on his desk pulled him from his reverie. He looked up to see one of his colleagues grinning at him. "Oi, Rob!" he called out, snapping his fingers to get his attention. "Stop daydreaming! You've been summoned by D!"

Snatch frowned. "Lester?" he mused. "What does he want now?"

He walked down the circular hallway that led to the office of the Director of Special Intelligence Service.

The corridor was lined with holographic displays and metallic panels that pulsed with a soft blue light, giving the space a cutting-edge, sci-fi feel. As he neared Lester's office, he saw Chief Adamson coming from the other end of the hall, her face set in a thoughtful expression. She was speaking to her aide as Snatch passed them.

"Alright, Jenkins," she said. "I'll leave the rest to you."

Snatch raised an eyebrow, intrigued by the odd interaction. The glass door to Lester's office opened to welcome him. The room was strikingly minimalist, with clean lines and a cool, metallic aesthetic that wouldn't have been out of place in a retro spy thriller. So Lester was committed to this type of aesthetic, Snatch thought.

"Director Lester," Snatch said as he entered, "you wish to see me?"

"Oh, Mister Church!" Lester's face lit up with a welcoming smile. "Please, have a seat."

Snatch settled into the chair across from Lester, trying to ignore his growing unease.

"Was that Chief Adamson and her aide I saw just now?" Snatch asked, trying to make sense of the situation.

"Yes, indeed," Lester confirmed, his smile fading slightly. "She came to submit her resignation."

Snatch's eyes widened in surprise. "Resignation? Why?"

Lester leaned back, his tone sombre. "It seems Chief Adamson was indeed aware of some covert operations Helix was involved in. She had her reasons for not disclosing it to the SIS, and as a result, she is taking responsibility for the failure in Hong Kong." His gaze softened a bit. "Her talent will be missed."

Snatch was taken aback. "That's unfortunate," was all he could say.

"Now that you're here," Lester continued, shifting gears, "I wanted to congratulate you on your excellent work. You've made significant strides in uncovering the truth behind the case."

Snatch felt a knot form in his stomach. "I was just doing my job, sir..."

The director's expression brightened as he pulled out an electronic folder from his desk. "As it happens, there is currently a vacancy for a Coordinator position in the Central Planning and Analysis Division. You should consider applying."

The folder's screen flickered to life, displaying details about the role. "I believe your skills and career would develop significantly in this role," Lester added.

Snatch glanced at the folder, his mind racing. The promotion was tempting, but his current situation made him wary. He wasn't sure if this was just a reward or if there were deeper implications he needed to consider.

"Thank you, sir," Snatch said cautiously, weighing his options. "I'll think about it."

Lester nodded, clearly pleased. "Good. Let me know your decision soon."

As Snatch left the office, the weight of the promotion offer felt heavy on his shoulders. How was he going to share this with Luna?

"Chief Adamson resigned?" Bishop's voice cut through a classic episode of *Rick and Morty*, disbelief evident in her tone, when he delivered the news.

They were in Snatch's living room, where he lazily flicked through streaming options on the flatscreen, barely paying attention. Meanwhile, she sat cross-legged on the floor, surrounded by a messy sprawl of documents and reports. She had raised concerns about the missing data on Orion, which was why she had chosen to work offline whenever possible. At first, he had found her method endearing, but now, as he looked at the sea of paper, he couldn't help but wonder how many trees had to be sacrificed for her paranoia.

"Yeah," Snatch replied, his gaze distant. "She's taking the heat for the mess that Helix left in his wake."

Bishop's eyes flashed with suspicion. "They're pinning Helix's actions all on her?"

Snatch leaned back, his thoughts jumbled. "Apparently she admitted knowing, from the start, that Helix was working as a Neo-Soviet asset."

Bishop recalled her last conversation with Chief Adamson, where she'd praised Helix highly.

"Helix has connections within the Guoanbu, as well as the triads and Russian mafia in Hong Kong. His extensive network will be invaluable for this mission."

Suddenly, it all clicked.

"Oh, God. She did it on purpose!"

Snatch looked confused. "What? Who?"

"Chief Adamson!" Bishop nearly shouted. "She deliberately let Helix work for the Soviets to gather intel that would weaken Jiang!"

Snatch still wasn't convinced. "How do you figure that?"

Bishop's voice grew intense, yet controlled. "If you think about it, it was an effective strategy for the Allies' benefit. Remember, Helix successfully exposed China's atmospheric seeding scandal and we managed to link Jiang to the triads in both Hong Kong and Taiwan."

"Yes, but now he is implicated in Jiang's shooting, and they're still digging into whether he had a hand in the murders of our agents in Hong Kong," Snatch cut in. "And don't forget, Adamson might not be as clean as you think."

"Snatch!" Her annoyance boiled over. "Do you really believe Adamson was trying to avenge her husband's death from more than 30 years ago?"

"I'm saying we need to consider all possibilities," he replied, trying to stay calm. "Your Chief had plenty of motive..."

"Motive?" Bishop's voice rose. "If we're discussing motives, isn't your Director the one who stands to gain the most from having his closest rival out of the picture?" Her tone was sharp, laden with accusation. With Adamson now sidelined, Lester finally had his chance to consolidate power.

Snatch's silence spoke volumes.

"I'm heading back," she said, sweeping up the scattered papers.

"Luna!" Snatch called after her, but she was already out the door, vanishing into the night, the unresolved arguments hanging heavily in the air.

As Bishop made her way home through the drizzling rain, she couldn't shake the turmoil inside her. Each step on the wet pavement seemed to echo her conflicted thoughts.

Sometimes, she wondered if everything that had happened in Hong Kong was just a dream. The whirlwind of betrayals and romance, the intensity of her connection with Helix and the life-threatening events they faced together seemed too surreal to be real. In the span of a few weeks, not counting her detainment, her world had turned upside down, leaving her heart aching with a strange longing even after her release. The memories of their stolen moments and shared vulnerabilities haunted her, making it impossible to forget him despite the chaos and uncertainty in her life now.

She hated how easily he had gotten under her skin, how just the thought of him could derail her purpose. Her rational mind told her to be objective, to weigh the evidence dispassionately, but her heart screamed otherwise.

Arriving at her townhouse, she shook off her umbrella and kicked off her wet shoes. Inside, she settled at her desk, the papers she had been working on spread out in front of her. She had intentionally kept her use of Orion limited to mundane tasks. The glaring gaps in the AI cloud's data made her suspect that something—or someone—was deliberately concealing the truth about what was really going on in Hong Kong.

This left her with only her offline notes and thoughts, some typed, some handwritten, to piece together the puzzle. As she stared at the documents, she began to type out her research.

Background:

Chief Adamson sent Helix and me to Hong Kong to investigate the murder of four British agents. The goal was to neutralise the suspects, believed to be Soviet operatives. A month later, Snatch discovered Helix's old codename on a list of Moscow's hired agents.

While trying to untangle the complex web of factions involved in Jiang's case, I've identified a few key players:

- Jiang, the radical president-to-be, shot but fine
- The Cheyevskaya Group in Hong Kong, led by a figure named Levski, who has strong anti-Soviet sentiments

- Zong Triad, the local Hong Kong syndicate, on friendly terms with Cheyevskaya and Safin
- Guoanbu's Third Bureau, the anti-Taiwan intelligence unit, now collaborating with Xiao Triad through Dragon Lady
- Xiao Triad from Taiwan, which seems to favour Taiwan's reintegration into China and is coddling up to Jiang

On the other side, you've got:

- Liu Xinhong, Jiang's political rival, who the Soviets are secretly backing
- Sluzhba station in Hong Kong, led by Kuznetsov
- The Fifth Column, Moscow's clandestine group that hires Western spies to do their bidding

These elements are like pieces of a puzzle that fit together in unexpected ways.

The leads so far:

Although Helix was always careful to omit sources in his reports, I know he received significant updates about these complex allegiances from Sylvia, the wife of Nicolai Politkov, Levski's heir apparent. Their exchange of information helps Sylvia protect her husband from rivals within Cheyevskaya, including Safin's nephew, Pyotr Dorodny.

Note about Sylvia: Before marrying Nicolai, Sylvia worked in finance and lived in several major European cities, including Amsterdam from 2028 to 2032.

Bishop stopped typing. Her thoughts drifted back to some of the things Helix had said.

"In '31, I was stationed in Amsterdam when I met an old friend from the military college."

"I knew Sylvia through a mutual friend… now, are you done with the interrogation?"

She tilted her head. Could Sylvia and their mutual friend be the key to understanding this mystery? She felt like she was onto something, but in order to confirm it, she had to dig deeper.

She finally decided to boot up the cloud, seeing the familiar Orion logo before her.

SIS AI Cloud / ORION

Hello, Agent Bishop. How can I help you today?

Leaning over her terminal, her fingers danced across the keys as she fed a series of prompts into the cloud. Her plan was simple: she would input unrelated inquiries about MI6 protocols, trivial details on past Hong Kong missions, and even obscure trivia about the Cheyevskaya's origins—anything that could muddy the waters. By filling the system with these red herrings, she hoped her real search queries, the ones that could potentially expose Helix's true connections with Sylvia, could be buried deeper within the layers of noise.

After spending a couple of days inputting random searches, she prompted: "Bundeswehr Command and Staff College, General/Admiral Staff Officer Course, 2018."

Orion loaded a list of participants on her holoscreen. The names appeared in neat rows, each accompanied by photographs of young military officers in crisp uniform. Brief summaries followed, outlining their branch of service, service history, academic performance, and notable achievements.

"Look up 2019 participants," she prompted next.

She worked methodically through the years, the sea of faces, all meticulously documented. She finally paused on a name, a face she recognised: Helix, or rather, the man who would become him, standing among his peers, eyes sharp even back then.

As she studied his young face and data in the military college records, she couldn't help but think he was rather cute, and for a moment, she wondered what kind of person he had been back then—before the layers of secrecy and betrayal had hardened him.

She caught herself daydreaming for a moment before shaking off the thought; there was work to be done. She needed to find the other key figure, the man who had crossed paths with Helix during those pivotal years. With a deep breath, she continued entering prompts, both relevant and irrelevant, as the rain pattered against her window.

14 / NEBEL

// Hong Kong //

Inside her fusion restaurant, Sylvia carefully arranged a bouquet of flowers on the counter. Her movements were precise, her attention fully absorbed in the delicate process. The soft fragrance of the blossoms filled the air, blending with the rich aroma of spices.

A waitress approached, clutching a small, neatly wrapped bundle of flowers.

"Miss, where should I place these flowers?"

"Over there, but separate the lilies," Sylvia replied without looking up. "The ambassador's wife is not fond of lilies."

The waitress nodded, ready to carry out the instructions when someone appeared at the door. The waitress approached the guest, an apologetic smile on her face.

"I'm so sorry, but we're not open to the public today."

The guest, however, remained firm. The waitress glanced back at Sylvia, silently asking for guidance.

Sylvia finally looked up from her flowers, her eyes narrowing as she recognised the woman standing at the entrance. It was Bishop, though her appearance had changed since last time—shorter hair, a trench coat draped over her frame, and heels that clicked softly against the floor as she stepped inside.

"If I'm not mistaken, 'Charlie', right?"

"Hi, Sylvia," Bishop responded, her voice low and steady. "Sorry to drop in unannounced."

They soon found themselves in Sylvia's luxury car, parked in a quiet corner near Victoria Harbour. The engine was off, leaving only the distant murmur of the city. Sylvia had rolled down the window to let in the cool breeze and was now puffing on a vape, its sweet aroma filling the air around them.

"So," Sylvia began, her tone light but probing, "what can I do for you?"

Bishop didn't waste time. "I'm sure you've heard about how Jiang's shooting had rocked UK-China relations… and that Alex is implicated in the incident?"

"Of course," Sylvia responded, exhaling a cloud of vapour. "Honestly, it's been a thorn on my side and Nicolai's."

"I believe Alex is innocent," Bishop said firmly. "And I'm trying to prove it. If you have any information or advice that could help..."

Sylvia's lips curled into a mocking smile. "As I recall, you didn't seem to like Alex that much. Why are you taking such a risk to defend him now? Did you finally fall for his charms?"

Bishop ignored the taunt. "He saved my life. He also made sure I wasn't caught up in his risky endeavours, even if it meant sacrificing his own safety... and freedom."

Sylvia tilted her head, eyes gleaming with something close to amusement. She leaned in closer, invading Bishop's personal space just enough to make her presence felt. "I see. So it was *he* who fell for your charms."

Setting herself back on her seat, Sylvia blew on her vape and looked away.

"Sorry, Charlie, but I'm not the person you're looking for. My relationship with Alex isn't that close. We've only been helping each other at the request of our mutual friend."

Bishop knew exactly who Sylvia was hinting at—their mutual contact, Helix's senior from the military college who went on to become a BND agent codenamed Nebel. Originally a double agent for Moscow, he had since evolved into a free agent with deep connections across various European intelligence networks. He also happened to be Sylvia's ex.

"Could this 'mutual friend' of yours help, then?" Bishop asked.

Sylvia's expression turned condescending. "Why would he get involved in this mess?"

Bishop didn't hesitate. "Maybe… because he was the one who first recruited Alex to work for the Soviets five years ago?"

Sylvia's demeanour shifted, the air between them growing tense. Leaning in closer, she spoke in a low, threatening tone. "Be careful what you say, Charlie. I don't associate with Moscow agents."

But Bishop wasn't backing down. "Don't pretend otherwise, Sylvia. Without the intel from Alex and his friend, your husband wouldn't have had the upper hand against Dorodny in front of Levski."

Sylvia's eyes flashed with anger, but instead of lashing out, she burst into laughter, the sound sharp and mocking. "You're incredible, Charlie! Do you really think empty threats will get you what you want? Remember this—debt is paid with debt, just as blood is paid with blood. Don't mistake the Cheyevskaya Group for a charity, got it?"

She pressed a button, and the door on Bishop's side swung open with a soft click. "Can you find your own way home?"

Bishop didn't flinch. She met Sylvia's gaze with a blank expression, then nodded. "Thank you for your time." She stepped out of the car and closed the door behind her.

"You're welcome," Sylvia replied coolly.

But before Bishop turned to leave, she bent down and spoke through the open window. "Sylvia, before I forget..." Her silhouette was backlit by the setting sun, giving her an almost ethereal glow. "Did Alex tell you he finally found proof Dorodny is working with Moscow?"

She walked away, but as expected, Sylvia opened her door, calling out after her.

"Charlie! Give me your number... and your real name. You don't look like a 'Charlie' to me."

Bishop turned around, a smile playing on her lips.

Bishop's boots crunched on the gravel path as she climbed Tai Mo Shan, each step pushing her further from the anxiety of her recent days. The hike was a welcome distraction, a chance to clear her mind after much waiting and uncertainty.

She paused at a clearing with a sweeping view of the valley below. Her phone buzzed, cutting through the tranquil silence. She glanced at the screen; it was an encrypted call, one she had been anticipating.

"*Bishop*," the man's voice was low and even, the faintest trace of a German accent colouring the words. "I understand you've been looking for me."

She wiped sweat from her brow and exhaled. "Nebel. Thanks for calling."

There was a faint chuckle from the other end. "You sound out of breath. Busy day?"

"Just keeping fit," Bishop replied with a snigger. Something about the man's cool confidence reminded her of Helix. "I need your help."

"So I've heard," he said with a hint of amusement. "You're in quite the predicament, trying to save a man who seems to attract trouble like a magnet. What makes you think I can help?"

"Because," she replied, choosing her words carefully, "if there's anyone who can pull the right strings, it's you."

He was silent for a moment. "You have a high opinion of my abilities. Unfortunately, the Fifth Column is no more, so there aren't many strings left to pull from here. However, if you uncover something of interest, I can make sure it gets to the right people."

"That's great," she said.

Nebel's voice took on a grave tone. "While I consider Alex like a brother, this isn't a favour. My involvement comes at a price. What you're asking isn't without risk—for me or for others."

Bishop's grip tightened on the phone. "Of course. Name your price."

She imagined his lips curving into a small, enigmatic smile as he replied, "You can't pay me with money or favours. I want your trust. Trust that whatever I do, you won't question it. And that you won't betray me for any king or country."

Bishop sighed deeply. This wasn't just a minor request; it meant unravelling her programming and abandoning her blind loyalty to her country—a step she knew would be irreversible once taken. "I understand," she said quietly.

"Good," Nebel said, a trace of approval in his voice. "And secondly, I expect you to do some of the legwork yourself."

She smirked. "I wouldn't expect anything less."

"Excellent," he replied. "Here's a clue: look into Taiwan."

She stood by the window of her hotel room, her gaze fixed on the setting sun as it cast a golden hue over Victoria Harbour. The sky was a gradient of oranges and purples, slowly fading into the darkening blue of night.

The situation weighed heavily on her; she had returned to Hong Kong with a purpose. Never mind that she was still under suspension and breaking every Crown rule by making illegal connections with foreign assets—even going as far as striking deals with them.

But at least, things were looking up. She had managed to engage the elusive Nebel and gained his trust somewhat. The other pieces of the puzzle were still scattered, but she would pick them up when she returned to London.

Standing in her hotel room now, she was reminded of the last time she and Helix were together, just before the operation at Phoenix Palace. They were watching the sunset from the apartment, rays spilling through the window just like they did now. She remembered how his arms had felt around her, the way his breath had tickled the back of her neck as they lay.

He had asked her, "Do you think you'll be a spy forever?"

She gave it a quick thought, but shrugged. "I don't know. I've never really thought about what comes after."

The words saddened him more than he cared to admit. "You've never thought about a life outside the Service?" he asked, "having a normal life, your own family one day?"

She met his gaze with a small, sad smile. "It's hard for me to imagine. Spooks like us don't usually get happy endings."

"You're a bit too young to be this pessimistic, Luna."

She chuckled, but saw the sorrow flickering in his eyes. As much as she wanted to ask him about it, something stopped her. It was fear—of what she might find if she pushed too hard, of confirming her growing suspicion of him.

They made love that night with a quiet intensity—which surprised both of them. She couldn't help but wonder if they had both known, even then, that their time together was running out.

Lying down on the bed, she closed her eyes and imagined his arms around her, his calloused hands exploring every inch of her. She trailed a finger along her collarbone, arching into her touch, cupping one breast then the other, thumbs brushing against sensitive nipples.

She unhooked her bra, letting it fall to the floor as she continued to undress. She ran her hands over her curves, imagining they were his. She pinched her nipples lightly, gasping at the jolt of pleasure that shot straight to her core.

The memory of that night was vivid in her mind's eye. She recalled taking him in her mouth, feeling his hardness deep in her throat, her tongue lapping at his head and tip while her palm stroked his testicles. He threw his head back, interlacing his fingers in her hair, guiding her as she bobbed up and down, sucking and slurping.

"Good girl," he had purred, which sent a rush of blood to her head and nether regions. He then grabbed her, lifting her body and turning her over like she weighed nothing. His face was right by her opening, and she felt his nose and tongue exploring, nuzzling into her core.

On the hotel bed, a soft moan escaped her lips as she pictured them mutually pleasuring one another. She slipped a hand beneath the hem of her underwear, fingers delving into her already damp folds.

The montage of titillating memories—the feel of his golden locks tickling her thighs, the delicious moans coming out of his lips as he rammed her, the friction of his length rubbing against her sensitive spots—brought waves of pleasure that crashed over her. Her touch quickened, panting his name against the empty room.

She lay sprawled across the bed, heart pounding, hair tousled from the pillow beneath. As the last ripples faded, she was left with an overwhelming emptiness.

No amount of self-love could compare; she yearned for his touch, his voice—anything to remind her he was real and not just a fleeting memory.

But for now, all she could do was wait, watching as the last light of day faded away, leaving her alone with nothing but the quiet, persistent ache in her heart.

15 / ENTRAPMENT

// London //

The radio played loudly in the background as Snatch stood at the counter, waiting for his order. The shop was filled with the savoury smell of roasting meat and frying potatoes.

GOOD DAY, LONDON! Rick Rose back with you on 95.8 KIS, along with the summer sunshine that's finally here! And now, here's the latest single from the legendary British rock band…

Khaled, the guy behind the counter, rang up the order and handed over two wrapped lamb kebabs with a side of chips and drinks in a large paper bag.

"That'll be 46.90, please."

Snatch scanned his phone to pay, protesting, "How is it more expensive every time I come here, Khaled?"

Khaled grinned. "Don't blame me, Rob! Abdul sets the prices!"

Snatch laughed, shaking his head. "If I'd known, I would've gone for some organic, healthy meal instead…"

"What's that supposed to mean? Kebabs are healthy!" Khaled shot back, and they both shared a laugh.

Making his way across town on transit, Snatch brought the lunch to Bishop's Whitechapel townhouse.

"Yo, Luna!" Snatch called out as he knocked on the door. "You home?" He found the entrance unlocked and grew concerned.

A voice came from inside, muffled but familiar. "In here, Rob. Sorry, it's a bit of a mess in here."

He pushed the door open, stepping into a living room that looked like it had been hit by a small tornado. Papers were strewn across the floor, empty wine bottles were scattered on the coffee table, and a general sense of disarray hung in the air.

"What's all this?" Snatch asked, looking around in disbelief. "You went dark for two weeks—what have you been doing? Do you even realise how damp this place is, and the alcohol stench—" he whizzed.

Bishop, sitting amidst the chaos, barely glanced up. "Sorry if my place doesn't suit your taste. But if you're only here to criticise, I've got a lot of work to do…"

Snatch wasn't having it. He walked over to the blinds and threw them open, letting sunlight flood the room. Bishop winced as the bright light hit her, the harsh reality of the beautiful day outside clashing with the gloom inside.

"Look at what you're missing," Snatch said. He moved to the glass doors, folding the panels open to reveal a small but lovely backyard. Finally, fresh air flooded into the room.

"Come on, let's eat," he suggested, holding up the food.

They sat outside on the deck, the sunlight filtering through the trees, casting dappled shadows. The aroma of the lamb kebabs lingered in the air. Bishop's eyes glazed as she picked at her mostly untouched food. Snatch, sitting across from her, took a bite of his chip, watching her with displeasure.

"Luna," he began, his voice cutting through the silence. "You haven't been eating or sleeping properly for days, have you?"

She barely met his gaze. "No, I haven't."

He chewed thoughtfully, already aware of the reason but letting her speak.

She leaned forward, her voice low and strained. "They're officially charging Helix with Jiang's assassination attempt. They're going to make an example of him. I'm running out of time."

Snatch sighed, pushing his kebab away. "Luna, have you ever considered… if he's really guilty?"

She looked up at him, her eyes hardening. "He didn't do it, Snatch."

"You're so sure," he said, his tone challenging. "But what if you're wrong? What if he really was playing us all along?"

Before she could answer, he added again: "Plus, even if he didn't do it, he was still being charged with the National Security Act—there was no way he was going to come out unscathed."

She argued: "Yes. But, since Helix is technically an agent of the Fifth Column, he wasn't really compromising any Crown secrets—his task from Moscow was to undermine China, after all."

Snatch gave a snort. "Do you think the higher-ups care about those details? Look, you've been driving yourself crazy over this. You're grasping at straws, and it's going to break you."

Bishop looked at him and finally smiled. "On the contrary, I came to an interesting lead on Jiang's shooting," she said.

Snatch's interest piqued, and he leaned in. "Oh?"

She went inside and called on Orion. The holoscreen displayed a map of Taiwan, alongside several images and documents.

"Taiwan?" Snatch questioned, raising an eyebrow.

"Yeah," Bishop replied, her fingers tapping around as she pulled up more information. "I've been so focused on Jiang and Helix's charges that I nearly forgot Dragon Lady also went on the seaplane that night."

She clicked through a montage of previous assassination attempts on presidential candidates. The screen flickered with images—past attempts on world leaders. Some of these attempts had bolstered campaigns, while others had backfired. Bishop pointed to a specific incident.

"In Taiwan, 2004," she began, her voice gaining strength as she recounted the events, "President Chen Shui-bian and his VP were shot while campaigning for re-election. Their injuries were minor, and they were released from the hospital the same day. They went on to win the election."

Snatch's eyes narrowed as he followed her train of thought. "Are you saying Jiang is trying to pull the same stunt? Using the tragedy to secure sympathy votes?"

Bishop nodded slowly. "I think so. But it goes deeper than that."

She clicked to a photograph that had stopped her cold the day before. A snapshot of the Dragon Lady, taken just weeks ago. She zoomed in on a stubbly man with slicked-back hair standing next to her.

Snatch squinted at the image. "Who is that?"

"Wan, also known as Julian Soh," Bishop snickered. "He looks different now, but I'm certain it's him."

Snatch's expression shifted to disbelief. "Soh the CIA agent? But he was killed in the Phoenix Palace shooting."

Bishop shook her head, her mind racing through the peculiarities that had nagged at her: the inconsistencies in the official reports, the unsettling way Soh had behaved during the Phoenix Palace incident.

"A dead man reappears, now linked to one of the most powerful figures in Taiwan's underworld. I'm starting to think he faked his death and defected, either to Taiwan or China—it doesn't really matter which. What matters is that I'm convinced he was involved in the fake assassination attempt."

She took a deep breath before continuing, "The entire operation was orchestrated by Jiang, with Dragon Lady's assistance. She wanted to prove her resourcefulness and cement their alliance. Their ultimate goal, of course, is the reunification of Taiwan into China."

Snatch stared at her incredulously. "...And how is this related to Helix?"

Bishop replied: "The Guoanbu knew about Moscow's secret directive to bring Jiang down using Western operatives. They found the perfect scapegoat to finally get rid of the Fifth Column."

She recollected events from the night at Phoenix Palace. "They set Helix up that night, luring him out. They also ensured the plan would go off without a hitch. For example, when I was trying to go after Helix, it was Soh who prevented and distracted me."

Snatch rubbed his temples in frustration. "OK, Luna, stop. This is wild, even for you."

She looked at him, defensive. "What is that supposed to mean?"

Snatch pulled out his phone and, with a few swipes, brought up the analyst feeds—endless streams of data and permutations compiled through Orion—all revolving around Jiang's assassination attempt, the sheer volume of information overwhelming.

He said: "Right now, the world's top analysts are scrambling to uncover the truth about Phoenix. This isn't the time for you to be spinning wild conspiracy theories without a shred of evidence."

Her laugh was harsh and defiant. "Conspiracy theories? Really, Rob? Just because I'm not an analyst doesn't mean I'm wasting my time."

"Oh yeah? Then where did you get these leads about Taiwan?" he demanded.

She hesitated, her face tense. "From an asset… a friend in Amsterdam."

Snatch's gaze hardened. "You mean, the former German agent who sold himself and Helix to the Soviets five years ago? The one you contacted while in Hong Kong last week?"

Her shock was immediate. "Are you spying on me?" she snapped, her voice rising.

"Of course I am!" he shot back, exasperation lining every word. "You're a suspended MI6 agent making illegal contacts with Moscow spies! I told you to steer clear of trouble. Are you trying to drag me down with your reckless behaviour?"

A pang of guilt showed on her face. Silence reigned in the room, but it was short-lived.

"Please, Luna," he pleaded, his voice softening but still laced with bitterness. "Stop this madness. All this damned obsession with Helix..."

"You think this is just about him?"

"Don't try to deny it! You haven't slept or bathed in days. You're wasting away and losing touch with reality. I don't understand what you see in him! If it is sex you want, I can give it to you—"

The accusation landed like a punch. Her slap was sudden and powerful, sending him stumbling backward.

"Is that how little you think of me?" she roared, eyes blazing with fury. "Do you really believe everything is that simple?"

Snatch staggered, hurt and shock etched on his face. He tried to speak, but Bishop cut him off. "You know, I've been asking myself the same question. Maybe I'm just pretending this is for a good cause! Maybe I'm wasting time and energy trying to prove a guilty man innocent! Maybe—maybe I'm just a foolish woman who was stupid enough to sleep with the enemy!"

She turned away and fixed her stare on her backyard.

"But then I realised..." she paused, her gaze distant, "do you remember that drive, that enthusiasm we both shared when we first met, when I joined the Service? Well, mine has long gone, as has my remorse and my conscience. I've been working solely to complete missions and, in the process, shut myself off all human emotions."

He didn't react, just sulkily rubbing his cheek. Bishop continued: "Strangely, since being suspended, I feel like I'm seeing the world as I used to. Not only do I feel free, I'm convinced that we can beat the system. So, even if I'm doing this only to help Helix or Chief Adamson, I don't care anymore. I'm just grateful to feel 'alive' again."

Snatch let out a bitter laugh, the exasperation giving way to a deep-seated weariness. "Well, isn't that lovely? Good for you to find peace in the middle of all this chaos." His voice dripped with sarcasm. "But don't drag me into it, not with the whole MI6 breathing down your neck."

He grabbed his bag, preparing to leave. "Have a nice life, Luna."

Her voice cracked as she called after him, "Rob! Why are you so cruel? Didn't we promise to always support each other no matter what?"

In a surge of raw emotion, he spun around, dropping his bag as he gripped her shoulders, eyes blazing with hurt. "Cruel? You're the one being cruel! You use me with your sweet words, never considering my position or my feelings. Do you have any idea what it's like to be treated this way by someone who claims to be your friend?"

Her breath hitched as the words sank in, the truth of them stinging. Tears welled up and began to spill down her cheeks. Unable to hold back any longer, she threw her arms around him. "I'm sorry, Rob. I… I just don't know who else I can trust in this world."

He hesitated, his hands hovering uncertainly before he finally embraced her, his grip tight and protective. He inhaled her scent, a mix of familiarity and longing overwhelming him. As he gently caressed her tear-streaked face, his expression softened, revealing the complex mix of emotions swirling inside him—concern, irritation, affection.

"Rob?" she murmured, her voice trembling with surprise and confusion.

He didn't answer. Instead, he silenced her with a kiss, his lips pressing against hers. His hands slid to the small of her back, pulling her closer as if trying to bridge the emotional chasm between them.

She felt desperation in the way he held her, the way his lips moved with urgency. The conflict within her deepened, her heart and mind at war. Finally, she hugged him tighter, kissing him back, torn between what she had planned and the betrayal she feared it represented.

She moaned into his mouth, knowing this was the right thing to do.

He woke up in her bed, the night heavy and silent around him. The sheets were tousled, her scent lingering in the fabric, but the bed beside him was cold and empty. He slowly sat up, rubbing his eyes.

Where has she gone?

In an attempt to shake off the remnants of sleep and the haze of the night, he reached for his clothes, slipping on his white shirt and jeans with a persistent sense of unease.

He had enjoyed every moment, every touch. She was beautiful, passionate. It had felt right in the moment, but now, he wondered if it would lead to awkwardness between them.

The house was eerily quiet as he moved through it, the only sound his bare feet padding against the wooden floor. Shadows stretched long in the dim light as he descended the stairs, the emptiness around him thickening with each step.

"Luna?" he called out softly, his voice barely cutting through the silence. "Where are you?"

A sinking feeling took hold as he scanned the darkness. *Surely, she's not regretting it already*, he thought to himself. The air—the house—felt wrong, as if it was holding its breath.

As he reached the bottom of the stairs, a sudden rush of air brushed past him, and before he could react, a heavy blow struck the back of his head.

Pain exploded in his skull, and the world spun violently out of control. The last thing he registered before everything went black was the cold, unforgiving floor rushing up to meet him.

When he regained consciousness, the first thing that came into focus was the light bulb hanging from the narrow ceiling. His vision doubled and blurred as he struggled to concentrate, gradually recognising the cold, barren surroundings of what appeared to be a basement. His hands and feet were tightly bound to a chair, the rough rope biting into his skin, leaving no doubt he was trapped.

He strained against his bonds, his heart pounding. In the far corner, someone hunched over the washing machine, a laptop open beside them, casting an eerie glow over the scene. His own phone was in their hand, the screen illuminated with data he knew all too well.

"Hey, mate," Snatch croaked, his voice hoarse, trying to summon some bravado despite his growing fear. "There's no point. All the data on that phone is encrypted, and there are three layers of protection to unlock it, which only certain MI6 personnel can access."

He forced himself to sound confident, knowing he had little leverage. "Let me and the girl go, and I'll give you the code."

The figure in the shadows slowly straightened up and turned to face him, stepping out of the darkness.

"Thanks for the offer, Mister Church," the voice said icily, "but I've got everything I need."

He recognised the voice instantly, but it was different—harder, devoid of the usual warmth.

Bishop stepped into the dim light. Her hair was pulled back in a short ponytail, and she wore a skintight compression top and leggings that accentuated her every movement, exuding an air of cold menace.

His breath caught in his throat as he took in the sight of her. "Luna... Why...?"

"Why? How about you explain this to me?"

Gone was the tenderness of earlier, replaced by something far more dangerous. She had used entrapment to draw him in, to catch him at his most vulnerable, and now she was ready to strike.

She stepped closer, holding up his phone, displaying several tabs filled with names and photographs—things she had pieced together while he was out cold. "Why did you hide this list from me?"

"What list?" he stammered, though he already knew the answer.

"The list of Moscow assets you found, which oddly enough not only includes Okto's name... but also the names of the four British agents who were killed in Hong Kong when this all started. You failed to mention that those dead agents were also listed as assets."

She leaned in casually, her demeanour calm yet unsettling. "Hey, Snatch. Why do you think it was Guoanbu that attacked Helix and me in the apartment? Is it because you knew they were after the fifth columnists all along?"

Before he could respond, her hand moved with a sudden jerk. She grabbed a fistful of his hair, yanking his head back with a practised motion, and pressed a knife against his throat.

Her voice carried a calculated fury that sent a chill down his spine. "Do you realise what this means? You knew it wasn't the Soviets who killed our agents. You knew someone was manipulating the data to pit us against them. And yet you kept this from me?"

Panic surged as Snatch felt the blade's cold edge against his skin. "W-wait, Luna! Don't jump to conclusions—"

She kicked the chair with brutal force, sending it crashing to the floor. The impact reverberated through the room, and Snatch's head throbbed with pain as he crumpled to the ground. Fear pooled sharply in his mouth.

"Don't even think about wriggling your way out of this!" Bishop's voice was a venomous hiss. Her anger seemed to build with every breath. "You knew those four dead agents were Soviet fifth columnists, just like Helix! Do you know how many people died because of your secrets? How many lives you've put at risk? You also let your own friend fight for their life in a hostile country... for what—a promotion and a pay rise?!"

Snatch struggled to lift his head, desperation etching itself into his features. His mind raced, trying to conjure any explanation that might defuse the situation. "No, that promotion... I didn't plan it! It was Lester—"

Before he could finish, Bishop's gun was in her hand. Her wrath had reached a fever pitch, her eyes blazing with fury. She crouched beside him, the cold barrel pressing against his temple.

"Was Lester involved in this, Snatch? Did Guoanbu kill those double agents? Was Jiang really the one who orchestrated his own shooting?"

Each question was a relentless assault, demanding answers that Snatch had no choice but to provide. "Talk or I'll pull this trigger!" Her voice was trembling with rage now, the threat in her tone unmistakable.

Fear rushed through him, and he blurted out, "Fine, Fine!! I'll talk!"

Bishop's grip on him loosened slightly, giving him a moment to catch his breath.

He began to speak, his voice trembling with a mix of fear and desperation. "It wasn't supposed to go this far," he said, his voice cracking. "I... I was given an impossible task by Lester."

Bishop's eyes narrowed, her voice dropping. "A task from Lester? You mean... to help him take down Adamson? Are you saying a petty personal ambition led to all this—deception, deaths, an international crisis?"

Snatch let out a strained laugh, his breath ragged. "You really don't get it, do you? Lester... he's just an old, washed-up spook who could never outmanoeuvre Adamson. He's got very little left—both in power and reach. Luckily, when he threw his mess my way... you showed up, asking about Soh. And without meaning to, you led me straight to his plan to defect to the Dragon Lady..."

Bishop's eyes widened. "Snatch," she snarled, grabbing his shirt and lifting him halfway off the ground, "You contacted Soh... and exposed Helix's identity to him?"

He smirked, a nervous laugh escaping as cold sweat trickled down his face. "Not just Helix's identity... Why do you think MI6's tight security system could be sabotaged during Jiang's shooting? Ironic, isn't it? The Phoenix incident couldn't have happened without Lester's approval..."

Before he could finish, she pummelled him with her fists, each punch landing with brutal force on his face. Blood spattered from his nose and mouth, but she didn't stop.

"You!! I'll fucking kill you all—WITH MY BARE HANDS!" she screamed, throwing him around like a rag doll to the wall, chair and all, her strength surprising even herself.

Finally, exhausted and trembling with exertion, she collapsed against a pillar, her chest rising and falling rapidly as she struggled to regain her breath. "Is there truly no principle, no shred of morality left in you people? For fuck's sake!"

Snatch, lying face down with blood trickling from his battered face, managed to turn his head to face her. His eyes, dark with guilt and something akin to sorrow, met hers. "It's pointless, Luna... no matter what you do, you can't stop them. They're far too powerful, and we're nothing more than small fry. All we can do is close our eyes and try to survive. See no evil, hear no evil, speak no evil..."

Bishop shot him a cold, unyielding look before standing up and striding over to him. She seized the chair from behind and yanked him upright, leaning in and whispered in his ear.

"Don't play the martyr just because your little scheme fell apart. Weren't you the one who always said there's an opportunity in every tragedy?"

She grabbed her laptop from atop the washing machine and set it on his lap. It wasn't connected to Orion, but to another cloud. Snatch's eyes widened in shock as he recognised the ominous red sphere and the stark, utilitarian interface of SFERA—the Neo-Soviet AI database.

Bishop dragged a chair in front of him and sat down, leaning forward with her elbows on her knees, her hands cradling her chin as she contemplated.

"Considering the thoroughness of the sabotage during the Phoenix incident," she began, her tone calm and analytical, "I suspect Jiang and the Dragon Lady had help from someone inside Guoanbu. There should be a paper trail, like an internal memo or authorisation for the operation. Can you use your skills and connections to find it?"

Snatch's face twisted in disbelief. "What? Even if that's possible—Even if we manage to prove that Jiang orchestrated his own shooting... Lester would never let that information go public! After all, he allowed the security lapse to happen."

Bishop's lips curved into a cold smile. "It won't be Lester's decision because we won't be the ones to release the news. We'll pass the evidence to our friend in Amsterdam. He'll ensure it reaches the right hands."

She looked up, still resting her chin on her hands, her expression cool and composed. "Consider this an apology to the Soviets for the loss of their agents in Hong Kong... and a gesture of goodwill from MI6 to maintain the Red Pact."

Her eyes locked onto his, still carrying a storm of antagonism, hurt and betrayal. Yet beneath it all, she understood him in a way that only years of shared camaraderie could forge. They were both caught in this tangled web, and they needed each other to survive.

She let the question hang in the air. "What do you say, Snatch?"

16 / EYES IN THE SHADOWS

SIS AI Cloud / ORION
SUMMARY: Aftermath of the Phoenix Palace Incident

Security clearance: Level 7
Report date: December 10, 2036
Attachment: SC-02102036-Helix

OVERVIEW

August 2036

- The scandal involving the engineered explosions and the shooting of Jiang Yaozu during the Phoenix Palace Incident (PPI) was exposed following the leak of an internal Guoanbu memo. Neo-Soviet sources were the first to discover this critical document. Despite China's swift formation of an investigation committee, the case was eventually dropped due to insufficient

evidence and internal political pressures.
- The involvement of the so-called 'Dragon Lady' of Xiao Group in Jiang's shooting remains a closely guarded secret, as does CIA agent Julian Soh's defection to Taiwan.

September 2036

- Despite the significant scandal during his campaign, Jiang Yaozu won the Chinese presidential election and was confirmed as the new leader. However, many political observers note that Jiang's nationalist policies have lost their previous resonance with the Chinese populace, leading to growing internal dissent and unrest.
- As China navigates its new political landscape, the UNSR, under a resurgent leadership, is poised to gain more influence within the Red Pact. This shift in power dynamics could impact international alliances and regional stability.
- John Hayward was appointed as the new Chief of Special Operations, replacing Leonor Adamson. Hayward's appointment

marks a significant shift in SIS's operational and strategic priorities.

October 2036

- The suspension of operative 'Bishop' / Special Ops was lifted. She has since been deployed on several short-term assignments, mainly counter-intelligence and anti-terrorism operations. Her return has been marked by a renewed commitment to operational integrity.
- SIS completed its investigation into senior operative 'Helix' / Special Ops. The findings confirmed his complex dual allegiance, though he officially retired from intelligence work under terms that include a non-disclosure agreement. *(Special Committee report attached)*
- The four British agents murdered in Hong Kong were identified as part of the Fifth Column, like Helix. These agents had been passing critical information to undermine Chinese nationalist movements, prompting Chinese intelligence to orchestrate their assassinations.

November 2036

- Operative 'Snatch' / Humint was appointed as the coordinator of the Central Planning & Analysis Division. His professional relationship with Bishop continues to be closely monitored by the SIS.
- An internal review is underway to assess the effectiveness of SIS's counterintelligence measures and to address any gaps exposed by PPI. This review includes evaluating the procedures for handling leaks and managing operatives with dual allegiances.
- SIS is also re-evaluating its strategic alliances and operational protocols in light of recent global shifts, including the rise of new political players and the evolving threat landscape.

Attachment: SC-02102036-Helix

SPECIAL COMMITTEE REPORT: Legal and Martial Decision on 'Helix' / Special Ops

BACKGROUND

Senior operative 'Helix' was implicated in an incident involving the shooting of Jiang Yaozu during the Phoenix Palace incident (PPI). This report outlines the disciplinary action decided against Helix for his breach of National Security Act and involvement in foreign operations.

INITIAL FINDINGS

Violation of the National Security Act (NSA)

Helix operated in close contact with Neo-Soviet agents as part of the 'Fifth Column'. While no direct UK secrets were compromised, his cooperation with a foreign intelligence service without prior authorisation from SIS constitutes a serious breach of NSA.

Motivations and Actions

Helix's primary mission from the Fifth Column was to counter Jiang's influence. This fact was known by his then-superior, former Chief of Special Operations Leonor Adamson. The committee acknowledges that his mission aligns with the Crown's broader strategic objectives, but this was not sanctioned by

SIS. Helix and Adamson's failure to report his Neo-Soviet affiliations have placed themselves and potentially UK interests at risk.

Operational Conduct

Helix's operational conduct raises serious concerns about rogue activities within SIS. Additionally, while employed by the SIS, Helix utilised resources in ways that support foreign powers, thereby leveraging Crown assets outside their intended scope.

SUBSEQUENT EVIDENCE

Exoneration from PPI

Further exposé and analysis efforts have substantiated claims that Jiang orchestrated events of the PPI. This exonerates Helix from his initial charges of being involved in Jiang's shooting.

Impact on National Security

While no direct UK secrets were compromised, Helix's cooperation with a foreign intelligence service is deemed to have indirectly influenced the current diplomatic tension.

DECISION

After careful deliberation, the Special Committee has reached the following decisions:

Suspension of Field Operations

Helix is to be immediately suspended from all active field operations. He will be reassigned to desk duties for a probationary period of 12 months. During this time, his actions and communications will be closely monitored.

Official Censure

A formal censure will be placed on Helix's record for violating NSA. This censure will include details of his unauthorised cooperation with Neo-Soviet agents and will serve as a permanent mark against his career progression within SIS.

Mandatory Counselling and Re-Education

Helix is required to undergo mandatory counselling sessions to address the psychological and ethical ramifications of his actions. He will also participate in a re-education program on the importance of adherence to SIS protocols, with particular emphasis on the dangers of unauthorised foreign collaboration.

Restricted Communication with Foreign Entities

Helix's communication with foreign entities, particularly those affiliated with Neo-Soviet interests, will be heavily restricted. Any interaction must be pre-approved by the new Chief of Special Operations and will be conducted under strict surveillance.

Review after Probation

Upon completion of the probationary period, Helix's case will be reviewed by the Special Committee to determine whether he is fit to return to active duty, whether further sanctions are necessary, or whether he should be permanently reassigned to non-field positions.

CONCLUSION

The committee acknowledges the complexity of Helix's situation, balancing his effectiveness as an operative with the need for accountability and adherence to SIS protocols. This disciplinary action reflects the serious nature of his infractions while recognising his contributions to broader strategic objectives. SIS remains committed to upholding the highest standards of operational integrity and security.

Signed:

- Director of Secret Intelligence Service
- Chief Legal Officer
- Deputy Director of Counterintelligence
- Chief of Personnel Affairs

End of Report
ORION / Eyes in the Shadows

17 / CHECKMATE

The sun had just begun to dip below the horizon over the manicured lawns of High Wigham Estate in Kent. The air was filled with the sound of laughter and clinking glasses as guests celebrated a wedding. Inside the estate's grand solarium, the atmosphere was much quieter.

Leonor Adamson, no longer the formidable Chief of Special Operations at MI6, sat at a small table in the centre of the solarium. A chessboard lay between her and an empty chair. She looked up as one of the estate's staff approached.

"Excuse me, Madam. Your guest has arrived."

Leonor nodded, a soft smile playing on her lips. "Please show her in."

A moment later, Bishop appeared from behind a wall of tangled vines, wearing a figure-hugging Roland Mouret dress, her hair up in a low bun. Her features softened slightly as she saw her former superior.

"Good evening, Madam," she greeted, her tone respectful but warm. Her face showed an odd mix of emotions. "How are you?"

Leonor stood and embraced her briefly. "Bishop! So good to see you again. Please, sit down."

Bishop took a seat across from her past mentor. "Thank you for the invitation," she said, glancing briefly at the elegant surroundings before her eyes met Leonor's again. "Why aren't you joining your niece and the groom outside?"

"I already did, but it seems I ended up boring the guests…" Leonor replied with a chuckle.

"You could never bore anyone," Bishop said.

Leonor waved a hand dismissively. "So, how have you been? Is the new Chief treating you well?"

Bishop hesitated for a moment before answering. "I've been well, and Chief Hayward is very supportive. But honestly, I still prefer working under you."

"No need to be polite," Leonor said, her eyes softening. She gestured to the chessboard. "How about a quick game?"

"Sure," Bishop said, though her brow furrowed slightly. "Though I don't really play that much…"

"That's all right," Leonor replied, pushing the board slightly toward Bishop. "You can go first."

Bishop thought of her opening move. She reached out, moving a pawn into position, the piece clicking softly against the board. They played in silence for a few moments, the game unfolding with an eerie resemblance to the world they both knew too well. The opening gambits, the careful positioning, the captures, the sacrifices.

During one turn, the former Chief said, "I'm sure you've often heard that managing intelligence agents is a lot like playing chess…"

"I think that is quite accurate," Bishop said thoughtfully, with a derisive smile. "But our game is much bloodier than just moving pieces on a board."

The warm light filtered through the solarium's glass roof, casting intricate patterns on the floor.

Leonor's gaze was steady as she moved another piece. "How long have you been working for MI6 now?"

"Not very long, about five years," Bishop answered as she thought of her next move.

"Is the world of intelligence so different from your military experience?"

With a touch of poignancy, she answered: "Yes, and I've only truly realised it recently.

"In the Army and the SRR, my primary focus was always the mission. We were trained to support each other as much as possible. But here, it's different. We're not just following orders; sometimes, our very presence can become part of the problem."

She paused, her fingers hovering over a chess piece. "Ironically, when I chose to defy the rules and follow my instincts, someone had already anticipated that move. In the end, I'm still just a pawn in this high-stakes game…"

"Bishop," Leonor said softly, "do you know why I sent you to Hong Kong?"

"I have a theory…" she answered.

"Let's hear it," the older woman encouraged.

Bishop took a deep breath, and reminisced the events of the past few months. "Suppose a group within MI6 felt threatened by your significant influence. When they discovered that your best operative had ties to the enemy, they immediately conspired to use that to bring you down. Add to that the escalating situation in China and the unsolved murders of our agents... You couldn't continue to refuse to deploy Helix to the field, even if the outcome was predictable."

Her mind's eye now replayed the two months she spent with Helix, from their encounter on the rooftop of a Moscow military hospital to their Hong Kong assignment, and their torrid affairs…

She brushed off the nagging feeling in her chest. "In that situation, I was your backup. Because of Helix's limited manoeuvrability, you needed a guarantee that the mission would still succeed. That's why you stoked the competition between us, even sending Helix to sabotage my last mission. So far, I can understand and accept that, Madam. But what happened afterward… is a different story."

Her voice grew intense. "It was bad enough that we were pitted against the Soviets, but then Helix broke his chain of command and turned against them—partially, I think, because of me. Meanwhile, your rivals were all too happy to sell him off to the Chinese."

She looked at Leonor, the woman she respected and admired, someone who had firmly established herself within the quaint, patriarchal stronghold of the SIS. "How did you manage to anticipate all these attacks on your own, Madam? The only asset you had on the field was an agent who knew nothing about the deeper conspiracies surrounding her. I didn't see the endgame," she admitted. "Not until it was almost too late."

"Don't feel guilty…" Leonor interrupted, "weren't you just being yourself?"

Bishop tilted her head, slightly startled by the question.

"At your core, you've always been a 'bishop', haven't you?" the former Chief continued, her tone reflective. "A bishop with strong convictions about the work you do. Loyal, reliable in both attack and defence."

She grabbed a black bishop from the chess board and held it up to the light.

"Often underestimated, a bishop can strike deep and far, with an elegant pattern of moves that often catch others off guard. Unfortunately, no matter how hard you try, a bishop can only cover half of the squares on the board. Without realising it, you've limited yourself from reaching your higher potential."

Bishop remained silent, but her widened eyes gave her away. Another black-and-white reference—was she really that easy to read?

Leonor continued: "You need someone who can show you the both sides to every story. Someone who is your complete opposite, who doesn't compromise, who is untouched by rules or convention…" her fingers picked up a different piece—the horsehead. "You need a 'knight'."

The analogy felt a bit too obvious, yet undeniably accurate. Helix was her knight—whether a dark knight or white didn't really matter. He had shown her that their world was woven from countless shades of grey.

Leonor began again: "In the beginning, you two were like oil and water. With clashing personalities and styles, you were challenged to outdo the other. But face that conflict, and when you manage to work together as a team… that's when the real game begins."

She put the knight back on the chessboard and called on the SIS AI cloud. "Orion, run simulation 1863."

A translucent holoscreen flickered to life on top of the chess board, displaying a dynamic simulation of a chess game.

The screen read:

`Rosanes Barred, Breslau, 1863. King's gambit accepted.`

Orion projected the game's progression with vivid clarity, capturing every detail of the board and the pieces in mid-air. Annotations followed the sped-up simulation.

In just a few moments, the board was down to half its original pieces. The black bishop and knight held the upper hand. The bishop, on a crucial diagonal, controlled key escape squares, while the knight, with its characteristic L-shape move, blocked any chance for the white king to escape. Though the white queen and other important pieces were still in play, they were rendered powerless.

`Bishop-Knight checkmate. Black wins.`

It was a classic endgame, one that demonstrated the near perfection of a well-executed strategy.

Bishop continued staring at the screen, the metaphor striking her with full force.

"You must know, Bishop," Leonor continued, "that the current MI6 leadership is getting old. Even if I were still there, how much longer would I stay? How much longer can Director Lester hold on? It's our duty to ensure the next generation understands how this world works. That's why I sent you to Hong Kong. Even knowing I might have to sacrifice a knight or even a queen…"

Bishop looked at the board, the pieces scattered, some sacrificed, others positioned for the final play. Her voice faltered. "I don't know what to say. I'm not sure I can ever repay you for everything you've done—"

Leonor cut her off, her fingers gently touching Bishop's hand. "It's alright, dear. Believe it or not, I also had my youthful ideals once. Back when I was the well-educated wife of a diplomat, we hoped to pass on all our worldly views to the younger generation. That time has long passed, but it's still fresh in my mind. I suppose every time I see you, I'm reminded of my younger self…"

Bishop's heart tightened at the words, but her lips curved into a slight, enigmatic smile. "You know what's funny, Madam? Someone else said that to me once, and I got really offended."

Leonor smiled back knowingly. "Could it be the person who asked me to give this to you?" She pushed a small envelope across the table.

Bishop reached for the envelope and opened it. It was an electronic boarding pass, Heathrow to Düsseldorf, bearing her real name, and dated for Christmas week.

"The holidays are coming," Leonor commented. "How about you take the rest of your leave from last year? If your new Chief objects, I'll have a word with him myself," she said with a twinkle in her eye, then sipped at her darjeeling.

The two women sat in a moment of comfortable silence. The world outside the solarium continued in its festive celebration, but within, there was a different kind of reflection, a quieter and deeper understanding between mentor and protégé.

18 / THE INVITATION

Luna stood in the cold, watching the snow fall gently onto the paved streets of Oberkassel. The well-off neighbourhood was dressed for Christmas, lights twinkling in the trees and wreaths hanging from every door. The air was crisp, her breath forming small clouds as she gathered the courage to knock on a townhouse entrance in front of her.

She had replayed the moment in her mind a thousand times since receiving the ticket from Chief Adamson, who had insisted that she start calling her Leonor. It had felt surreal, like a lifeline tossed to her in the midst of confusion. And now, here she was, her hand trembling slightly as it rose to knock.

The door opened sooner than she expected, and she found herself looking down at a small blond boy, no older than five or six. His eyes—eerily familiar—were a striking blue. He peered out, curiosity in his gaze.

"Hallo," he said softly, clutching a train compartment in his hand.

"Hello," Luna replied. She knelt to his level, her heart swelling at the sight of him. "Are your parents home?" she asked in broken German.

Before the boy could answer, a chiding voice came from inside the house.

"Lukas, I told you not to answer the door without an adult," The voice was unmistakable—rich, deep, and laced with the weight of memories that tugged at her heart.

Alex appeared in the doorway. He looked just as she remembered, though his hair was cut shorter, and the ordeals he had faced in the last few months had etched soft new lines into his face.

"Luna," he breathed, as if her name were a prayer.

"Hi, Alex," she said, standing up slowly, feeling suddenly self-conscious. "I got your ticket. I hope I'm not intruding..."

"Not at all," he replied quickly, stepping aside to let her in. "Please, come in. It's freezing out there."

She stepped into the warmth of the foyer, shedding her coat and scarf. The space was cosy, decorated with simple Christmas ornaments and the soft glow of a fire crackling in the hearth. Lukas watched her with wide eyes, and Luna couldn't help but smile at him.

"This is Lukas," Alex said, resting a hand on his son's shoulder. "Lukas, you can practice your English with Luna, OK?" he encouraged.

"Nice to meet you," Lukas said in English, his soft accent endearing.

Luna's earlier uncertainty melted away. "Nice to meet you too," she replied.

Alex gently removed her jacket, while Lukas, eager to help, looked up at his father for instructions.

"Can you help Luna with her luggage?" Alex asked.

As the boy scurried off with Luna's bag, a sound pinged from the kitchen, drawing Alex's attention.

"Oh, I've got to check the roast," he said. "Could you lend me a hand?"

She looked at the spatula in his hand, and at the red-chequered apron he wore that gave him a domestic aura. She giggled, lifting her sleeves slightly as she followed him into the kitchen.

The warmth from the oven greeted them as Alex carefully opened the door, a small puff of smoke escaping. The smell of the roasting ham filled the air, a tantalising mix of herbs and spices.

Lukas re-entered the kitchen, his shyness returning as he leaned against the counter. Luna caught his eye and smiled, her curiosity growing about this unexpected evening. As the roast finished, she helped Alex carry the potatoes and vegetables to the dining room.

"Dinner is ready!" Alex called out.

The remnants of dinner lingered in the air as the cosy warmth of the living room settled around them. Lukas was busy showing Luna all his toys and the electronic displays of some arts and crafts projects he had made in school.

His latest favourite toy, however, was the train set in the living room, which he had constructed from a kit over the past few days—with the help of his father, of course. The soft chugging noises filled the space as he lost himself in play.

Luna sat in an armchair, her thoughts drifting as she watched Lukas's earnest concentration. Alex approached her, a glass in hand.

"Vodka and lime soda, *fraulein*?"

Luna looked up at him, accepting the drink with a grateful smile. "*Danke*."

"Are you still day drinking during missions?" he teased.

Responding to the taunt, she snickered, "I've been cutting back, actually."

She glanced over at Lukas, still engrossed in his train set. "Your son is adorable, and looks like he's going to make a great engineer."

"Thank you," Alex replied with fatherly pride. "He's with me for Christmas this year." There was sadness in his eyes. "It's a pity I don't see him that often."

Luna turned to him, curious. "He told me he lives with his mother and stepdad in Munich."

He nodded. "Yes, almost exclusively. It's... much safer that way," he admitted.

Her mind buzzed with more questions than she dared to ask. She had found out some details about Helix's life after leaving the Service, that he'd started looking into work as a security consultant. But that didn't explain how he could afford a townhouse in Düsseldorf's most affluent neighbourhood. She suspected he had come from money, after all.

The more she dug into his post-MI6 life, the more inconsistencies she found. After Helix was exonerated for Jiang's shooting, it looked like the Service was keen to brush off his double agency with a mere slap on the wrist. Perhaps it was easier to let him slip into the civilian world and claim it was all resolved rather than admit how deeply compromised their operations had become.

The room remained quiet, the only sound being the soft clatter of the toy train on its tracks and the crackle of the fireplace. Alex sat down in the armchair across from her.

The silence was heavy, laden with the things they hadn't said since Hong Kong.

"I haven't properly thanked you for getting me out of detainment," he finally said. "I'm sorry for all the trouble, having you strike a deal with both the Cheyevskaya *and* Lester's cronies within MI6… I don't know how you managed it."

She shook her head, brushing off his apology and gratitude. "No need to thank me. I got a lot of useful information from your mission reports in Hong Kong. Without them, I wouldn't have been able to convince Sylvia, or Nebel. He was the one who tipped me off about Taiwan and how much deeper the conspiracy ran."

Alex looked amused. "I'm even more impressed you managed to win Nebel over. He's talked about you."

Luna giggled, "He reminds me of you—a great deal, actually. Now that I know how to handle your type, winning him over wasn't too difficult."

Alex smiled but knitted his brows slightly, half-wondering if he should be jealous.

She added, her voice tinged with sadness: "But honestly, it was the least I could do, especially since I was the one who handed you over."

He gently took her hand in his. The touch was warm, comforting. "You didn't have a choice," he said softly. "And you got detained as well. I hope they weren't too rough on you."

Her heart ached as she interlinked her fingers with his. "They weren't. But what exactly did they do to you in there?" She could only imagine his interrogation had been many times more severe than hers, and for much longer.

He gave her a reassuring smile. "I did go through a tough 're-education', as they called it. But, time heals all wounds. Even this one," he said, tapping on his left shoulder.

His eyes then turned to Lukas. "Besides, if I'm being honest, I was relieved to be out. This civilian life isn't so bad. I get to spend more time with family, and I'm getting better at cooking, too."

Luna knew that wasn't the full story. Surveillance on the former Agent Helix hadn't stopped, not by a long shot. MI6 might have officially let him go, but they hadn't truly released their grip. They were always scrutinising, waiting for him to slip up—or simply making sure he never became a threat again.

Despite all this, she chuckled. "You were right."

"About what?"

"There's a lot I don't know about you," she said, remembering his words the last time they were pouring their hearts out in a dingy room in Chungking Mansions, which felt like a lifetime ago.

Alex's eyes bore into hers. He did not tell her that there wasn't a day that went by that he didn't think about what happened, or about her.

"I think it's quite the opposite, Luna. I hardly know you at all," he admitted. "But, I know you're doing well at work, to the point that your new Chief was so hesitant to let you go for Christmas…" His eyes sparkled with a touch of humour.

She blinked, caught off guard. "Did Adamson tell you all this?"

His response was a hearty laughter. He got up and approached Lukas, encouraging him to start packing up and getting ready for bed—as he had a big day of opening presents tomorrow.

Luna couldn't help but feel a sense of warmth as she watched the father and son interact. The simple domesticity of the moment gave her a rare glimpse into a life that had been, and could just be.

The hallway was softly lit as Alex stood by Lukas's bed, the boy's room filled with gentle Christmas reverie. Lukas, already tucked in and looking cosy under his blankets, gazed up at them with sleepy eyes.

"Sleep well," Alex said softly, "we'll open your presents first thing in the morning."

Lukas gave a small, contented smile. "Bye bye, Papa. Bye, Luna," he added, his voice a sleepy murmur.

Luna waved her hand from the doorway. "Good night, Lukas. Sleep tight."

With a final tender look, Alex stepped out, the soft click of the door closing behind them. They walked a few steps before he turned to her, a thoughtful expression on his face.

"I forgot to ask," he said, "how's your friend Snatch doing?"

Luna rolled her eyes at the mention of the name. "He's doing well, he's already planning his next promotion. Like him or hate him, he knows how to play the game. And he is proving quite helpful… most of the time."

A smirk tugged at the corner of Alex's lips. "Is that so? Because I heard he had a thing for you."

Luna laughed, shaking her head. "Not anymore! I'm done dealing with double and triple agents."

His grin widened as he took a step closer. "Well, I hope you're not cosying up to your new partner either."

She scowled. "Seriously, what do you take me for?" Her thoughts drifted back to Hong Kong, to the moments that had brought them together and then torn them apart. It was a series of circumstances that made her go against her grain, and there was no way she was going to repeat it again.

There was no one quite like you, Helix.

"Besides, didn't Chief Adamson tell you I've been working alone?" she teased.

He leaned in even closer, his voice dropping to a low murmur as he brushed a strand of hair away from her face. "No. But, Leonor mentioned your next mission isn't until mid-January. Does that mean you'll be staying here until the New Year?"

Luna felt a warmth spread through her chest. So this was why her ticket had an open return date.

"Hmm," she replied, tilting her head up, "that depends."

His expression was caught between amusement and curiosity. "On what?"

She batted her eyelashes. "On whether or not you can stop bragging about your closeness with Leonor."

He chuckled, a deep, rich sound. "Are you really jealous this time?"

She bit her lip, the teasing banter making her heart race. "Well..."

Before she could finish her line, they locked lips, his strong hands on her waist and her grip on the back of his neck, pulling each other closer.

Their connection was as electric as it had ever been. Every emotion they had held back, every moment they had missed, bound them in a way that words could never express.

When they broke apart to catch a breath, he rested his forehead against hers, his voice a low whisper. "I've been wanting to touch you since dinner... to hold you close."

Her fingers traced the line of his jaw as she looked into his azure eyes, finding the same longing reflected back at her. "Then don't stop," she purred.

It was easy to see that the dynamic between them had shifted. Once Luna allowed herself to finally trust him, the sharp edge that underlined their previous relationship had morphed into something deeper, more genuine.

No longer burdened by suspicion, the pressure to prove herself, nor the gnawing guilt that she was possibly sleeping with the enemy, the new Luna was a lot more liberated, playful... and daringly provocative—not that Alex minded.

After a day of exploring the city and enjoying the Christmas market with father and son, she found the perfect moment to give Alex his holiday gift: herself, draped in an enticing mix of sheer mesh and lace.

At midnight, she showcased the lingerie with a sultry smile. The lace cups pushed up her breasts, barely containing them, with nipples peeking out of the sheer mesh. The bottom was a daring thong crafted from the same red material that left little to the imagination. It dipped into a seductive V-shape, drawing his eye downward.

His first instinct after admiring the garment was to either take it off or tear it all apart, but she stopped him, bending over and showing him the teasing slit that ran along the centre instead.

He didn't need any encouragement as his hands found her waist from behind, bringing her close to him, his erection teasing her entrance. His fingers traced down her skin, exploring her curves, then slipping between her folds. When his hardness finally entered her, she let out a quiet gasp, adjusting to the familiar, intoxicating stretch.

As he started moving inside her, he realised that he had changed too. For him, it was the satisfaction of finally being with someone who truly saw him and accepted him without pretence—no secrets, no lies, just a rare, undeniable connection that manifested in an insatiable desire for every part of her: mind, soul, and definitely body.

He loved that she was keen on giving him control, knowing he would take her to the limits of pleasure while still keeping her safe. He pulled on her hair, creating a beautiful arch of her back while their hips met in a rhythm as primal as it was passionate. Her moans turned into muffled screams into the sheets as he continued pounding, taking her with animalistic ferocity.

As much as she loved being rammed from behind, him hitting all her pleasure spots, she longed to see and touch more of him. A side glance from her was all it took for Alex to understand. He broke off their rhythm mid-thrust, turning her around to face him.

"I want to taste you," she whispered, dropping to her knees without warning. She took him into her mouth, purring in appreciation as she looked up at him through her lashes.

But he would have none of it—he needed her back with him, close, connected. Sitting at the edge of the bed, he stroked himself, commanding her without words to climb on top. She complied, climbing up and resting on his thighs with spread legs.

Soon, he was inside her again, each thrust punctuated by the sound of wet flesh slapping together. Sweat was slicking their skin while their mouths and tongues were busy kissing, tugging, nibbling.

She dug her nails into his back, her muscle-bound Adonis with the face and hair to match. His calloused palms fondled her all over, finally settling on her hips, gripping them hard enough to leave bruises.

As his powerful thrusts drove her closer to ecstasy, hearts pounding in sync, an unfamiliar warmth bloomed in her chest. It was more than just the physical pleasure coursing through her veins; it was a tender ache that made her want to hold him closer, keep him inside her forever.

He felt it too, his rhythm faltering as their eyes met. In those dark depths, he saw something stirring beyond lust—a vulnerability that mirrored his own. He slowed down, burying his face in her exposed breasts, suckling on her nipples through the slinky mesh.

She responded with a whimper, wrapping her arms around his neck, and they moved together now not just with urgency but with an emotion that was harder to name, yet undeniably present.

When the orgasm crashed over her like a wave, she clenched around him, milking him as he followed suit with a guttural groan. They collapsed together on the mattress, panting and sated.

They locked eyes again, her dark gaze meeting his icy blue one with an intensity that made the world around them fade away. The words slipped out before she could think or stop them.

"I love you," she breathed against his mouth. The confession tumbled out with a vulnerability that startled her. For a split second, panic gripped her. What if this was too much, too soon?

But before the fear could take hold, Alex's response came, steady and sure, anchoring her in a way that only he could.

"I love you too," he replied, his voice steady and certain as he leaned in to kiss her. In that kiss, she felt the truth of his words, the depth of his feelings, and the unshakable connection they shared. "Maybe since Hong Kong."

Her heart fluttered, just like it had when they first met. Memories of their mission together surged through her—every stolen glance, every heated exchange, every time she'd felt that undeniable pull toward him. In this moment, completely lost in each other, a sense of peace washed over her, as if nothing else in the world mattered.

The kitchen was bathed in morning light, a warm glow settling over the remnants of another intoxicating night. Luna sat at the table, her legs casually crossed under the shirt she'd borrowed from Alex. It hung loosely on her, the fabric just grazing her bare skin.

Across from her, he was engrossed in his breakfast, his every move deliberate and unhurried. The light caught the golden strands of his fringe, the love marks she had left on his neck, and also the large scar on his shoulder, a stark reminder of how close he'd come to not making it out alive.

They ate in near silence, the only sound the clink of cutlery against plates as they made their way through an English-German breakfast: eggs, bacon, beans and bratwurst.

Luna's gaze strayed to the scar on her own left thigh, the one left by Vareleva. The quiet between them was comfortable, but beneath it, her mind was churning. The holidays were over, Lukas was back in Munich with his mum, and soon she—or rather, Bishop—would have to go back to work.

She pushed her plate aside, breaking the silence with a soft, measured voice. "I've booked my flight back to London." The words hung in the air. She looked at him, searching his face for any sign of unease. "Do you… want to have that 'talk' you mentioned back at Phoenix Palace? About this 'thing' between us?"

Alex paused, a faint smile playing at the corners of his mouth as he met her eyes. "No," he replied, his tone laced with a lazy confidence. "I don't need the talk. I'm not going anywhere."

The simplicity of his words should have been reassuring, but Luna felt a small knot tighten in her chest.

"But I'll be away for long periods of time," she pressed, concern slipping through. Relationships weren't supposed to be fragmented, with endless stretches of absence. She had been down this road before, only to be disappointed.

He leaned back in his chair, still relaxed. "I know," he said, a hint of the past flickering in his eyes, "I've been on the other side too, when Anna left because I was hardly ever home."

The memory of that heartbreak cast a brief shadow over his face. "But I'm different… we're different. We understand the world we come from, and the demands it places on us."

He smiled, the genuine kind that reached his eyes. "For now, I'm good with what we have… as long as you're not sleeping with your new partner—or enemy."

The smile morphed into a familiar smirk, his eyes flashing with that blend of humour and challenge that had always kept them on their toes.

Luna scoffed, a smile tugging at her own lips. "You're impossible," she muttered, half exasperated, half amused by his unshakeable confidence.

He tilted forward, reaching across the table to link her fingers with his. As ever, his touch was electric, sending a shiver down her spine.

"Don't worry about me," he murmured, his voice dropping to a low, almost conspiratorial tone. "I'm busy too. I've got some leads for the new 'consulting business'. VIPs, private security contracts, a little corporate espionage here and there. You know, the usual."

His tone was smooth, almost dangerous, as if he were discussing something as mundane as the weather. "We might even cross paths in the field one day."

She raised an eyebrow, the prospect both thrilling and slightly nerve-wracking. "Really? And what if we're on opposite sides?"

He didn't miss a beat. Leaning closer, he let his fingers find her lips, his touch possessive and tender all at once. His voice was a husky whisper, filled with a dark, playful promise.

"Then I guess we'll see who's better at playing the game."

EPILOGUE

Bishop stood on the rooftop of her townhouse, the January morning air crisp against her face. Wrapped in a long white parka, she cradled a cup of tea in her hands, the steam rising and mingling with the cold breath of the city.

This was her ritual, a moment of calm before the chaos. Her mind was spinning with details of the next mission that Chief Hayward had briefed her on yesterday, but she resisted. This was no time for planning; she needed to reflect, to anchor herself in the lessons of the past year before diving into what was to come.

She took a sip of the tea, savouring the warmth as it spread through her. As she tried to continue her introspection, her thoughts kept slipping to Helix—Alex. The memory of his touch, the sound of his voice, the way he felt inside her—

Not now. She forced herself to push those thoughts aside, to focus on the here and now.

This past year had taught her more than she ever imagined. It had pushed her to her limits, made her question everything she thought she knew, and forced her to grow in ways she hadn't anticipated. She had learned to navigate the murky waters of trust, to balance duty with desire, and to face her fears head-on.

The world around her continued to change, too. Alliances were shakier, threats more insidious. The very fabric of the world and the climate seemed to be unravelling, and in its place was a landscape that was both terrifying but full of potential.

The wind blew her hood open as she gazed out over the city she called home. The world below might never know the risks she took, the battles fought in the shadows to keep the peace. But she didn't need recognition or praise. All she needed was the drive, the purpose, and the knowledge that she was doing what she was meant to do.

Her thoughts drifted back to the next mission. She still needed to arrange that dinner with Snatch to secure the information and contacts he had promised her. In this world, she had learned to keep her few friends close—especially those who could give her an edge.

She smiled softly, the weight of the world not quite so heavy on her shoulders. Whatever the future held, she was ready to face it, not as a pawn in someone else's game, but as a queen in her own right.

With one last look at the city, she finished her tea and headed back inside, ready to begin again.

POSTSCRIPT

SIS AI Cloud / ORION
SURVEILLANCE REPORT: Rolf Alexander Richter (formerly 'Helix' / Special Ops)

Security clearance: Level 7
Commissioned by: Michael Lester, Director of Secret Intelligence Service
Prepared by: Robert Matthew Church, Senior Coordinator of Central Planning & Analysis Division
Report date: May 15, 2037

SUMMARY

Despite Richter's official resignation from SIS after his exoneration last year, surveillance on him remains active. Richter, previously senior operative 'Helix' of the Special Operations Division, has successfully transitioned into the private sector, specialising in high-level security consultancy and corporate espionage.

KEY FINDINGS

Professional Influence

Richter's consulting venture is attracting elite clients, including multinational corporations and high-profile individuals. His influence in security and intelligence circles persists, indicating a potential for continued significant impact.

Professional Connections

Richter's network reveals close ties with former agents of the now-defunct 'Fifth Column', a Moscow-backed faction known for its clandestine operations. His connections with these ex-agents suggest an ongoing association with Neo-Soviet and other hostile intelligence agencies.

Personal Connections

Of particular interest is Richter's ongoing involvement with senior operative 'Bishop' of the Special Operations Division. Surveillance indicates that their relationship extends beyond professional interactions into a deeply personal and intimate affair.

RECOMMENDATION

Continue to monitor Richter closely, with particular attention to his interactions with Bishop. The personal nature of their relationship and its implications for both their professional roles and SIS operations warrant sustained vigilance.

End of Report

It's the oldest question of all, George.
Who can spy on the spies?

John le Carre,
"Tinker, Tailor, Soldier, Spy"

Thank you for reading 'Bishop's Gambit'.
Agent Bishop will be back in 'Bishop's Capture'.

If you could spare a moment, please consider leaving a review.

Amazon

Goodreads

ABOUT THE AUTHOR

I like to craft tales that transport readers into enchanting worlds, whether rooted in forgotten histories or set in post-apocalyptic futures. At the heart of it all are unforgettable characters and timeless passions that linger long after the final page.

In my previous life, I was a journalist, a travel writer, and a manga artist. I was born in Southeast Asia and now call the Canadian prairies home with my husband and two children.

Say hello on Instagram, Facebook or Tiktok:
@samaraknightauthor

Join newsletter for new releases and giveaways:
www.samara-knight.com

ALSO BY SAMARA KNIGHT

Bishop's Capture

Bishop knows no one is coming when she is captured, cut off from allies and left for dead. Her only hope? Her boyfriend and former partner, now a private mercenary with questionable loyalties. (Shadows & Secrets #2)

Bishop's Endgame

For the ultimate spy couple, happily ever after may be the toughest mission yet. (Shadows & Secrets #3)

The Viking Wanderer

An epic tale of an Icelandic blacksmith who falls from the sky and finds himself stranded in a quaint Chinese village. (Rift Odyssey #1)

The Flowering Knight

As spring blooms in her twentieth year, gifted silver-smith Ai meets a dashing Sillan nobleman who sets her world alight. (Rift Odyssey #2)

Manufactured by Amazon.ca
Bolton, ON

45095961R00187